THE TALNIKOV FAMILY

THE TALNIKOV FAMILY

A Novel

AVDOTYA PANAEVA

Translated by Fiona Bell

Columbia University Press
New York

Columbia University Press wishes to express its appreciation for
assistance given by the Pushkin Fund in the publication of this book.

Columbia University Press
Publishers Since 1893
New York   Chichester, West Sussex
cup.columbia.edu

Library of Congress Cataloging-in-Publication Data
Names: Panaeva, A. ĪA. (Avdotʹia ĪAkovlevna), 1819–1893, author. |
Bell, Fiona (Translator), translator.
Title: The Talnikov family : a novel / Avdotya Panaeva ;
translated by Fiona Bell.
Other titles: Semeĭstvo Talʹnikovykh. English
Description: New York : Columbia University Press, 2024.
Identifiers: LCCN 2024006971 (print) | LCCN 2024006972
(ebook) | ISBN 9780231213189 (hardback) | ISBN 9780231213196
(trade paperback) | ISBN 9780231559768 (ebook)
Subjects: LCGFT: Novels.
Classification: LCC PG3337.P24 S413 2024 (print) | LCC PG3337.
P24 (ebook) | DDC 891.73/3—dc23/eng/20240308
LC record available at https://lccn.loc.gov/2024006971
LC ebook record available at https://lccn.loc.gov/2024006972

Cover design: Henry Sene Yee

CONTENTS

INTRODUCTION

AS REVOLUTIONARY UPHEAVAL spread through Europe in 1848, the Russian writer Avdotya Panaeva launched her own attack on a powerful institution: the family. Like the political uprisings of the time, *The Talnikov Family* was promptly suppressed, the censor blocking publication by calling the novel "cynical" and "undermining of parental power."[1] He was right: with equal parts humor and rage, the novel's narrator recalls her violent girlhood in an abusive household in Saint Petersburg. Natasha's father whips his children but lavishes attention on his many birds and dogs. Her unmarried aunts take their disciplinary measures, and their toilettes, to ever more ridiculous extremes. Meanwhile, Natasha and her siblings conspire in games and revenge plots, stealing back the joys of childhood wherever they can find them.

Panaeva was twenty-seven when she wrote *The Talnikov Family*. Ten years earlier, she could hardly have imagined a future as a published author. Born in 1819 to Yakov Bryansky and Anna Bryanskaya (née Stepanova), two actors in Saint Petersburg's imperial theater, Avdotya was raised in a chaotic household where children's physical, emotional, and educational needs were entirely neglected. At eighteen, while training as a ballerina, Avdotya managed to escape this domestic hell by eloping with the nobleman and writer Ivan Panaev. His family opposed a match with a girl from a family of performers, and in some sense their concerns were well-founded: Panaeva herself could not have anticipated how central a role class antagonism would play in the rest of her life. Traveling for the first time to her new husband's country estate, Panaeva attended a will-reading of Panaev's relative, which ended in enserfed families parceled out to different family members and separated forever. Raised in the urban capital, Panaeva was shocked to witness the violence of serfdom and to find herself suddenly a member of the enserfer class.

Nearly a decade into what proved to be a dissatisfying marriage, Panaeva was introduced to another new world. In 1847, apparently at her urging, Panaev and the poet Nikolai Nekrasov bought the defunct literary journal *The Contemporary*—once overseen by the poet Alexander Pushkin—and began publishing prose and criticism of a liberal inclination. The Panaevs' apartment served as the editorial office, and Panaeva hosted the journal's renowned contributors, including Vissarion Belinsky, Ivan Turgenev, Lev Tolstoy, and Fyodor Dostoevsky. Despite being denied a formal education, Panaeva suddenly found herself at the center of the liberal Russian literary scene.

"None of the writers knew that I wrote," Panaeva recalls. She coauthored the fashion column with her husband, but the men thought of her as a hostess more than anything else. In 1848, when *The Talnikov Family* was being prepared for publication in the *Illustrated Almanac*, a limited-edition book for subscribers to *The Contemporary*, the revered critic Belinsky read the manuscript and demanded that Nekrasov reveal the identity of the author, some "N. Stanitsky." After Belinsky discovered the bearer of this male pseudonym, he rushed to Panaeva's apartment. She recounts their exchange in her memoirs:

> "At first I didn't want to believe Nekrasov when he told me it was you who wrote *The Talnikov Family*," he said. "Aren't you ashamed to have not started writing earlier? No one in literature has ever touched on such an important issue as the relationship of children to their guardians and all the outrages that poor children endure. If Nekrasov hadn't named you, but had demanded I guess which of my female acquaintances had written *The Talnikov Family*, then, I'm sorry, but I would never have thought that it was you."
>
> "Why not?" I asked.
>
> "Well, you have this look about you: always busy with the household."
>
> I laughed and added:
>
> "And after all I'm always only thinking about clothes, as everyone says."
>
> "Sinner that I am, I also thought that you only had clothes on your mind. Yes, to hell with them, write, write!"[2]

Panaeva apparently gave Belinsky her word. She would continue to write, both independently and with coauthors, for the rest of her life.

Panaeva's years at *The Contemporary* were by turns thrilling and exhausting. Her writing was consistently edited and published, and she had considerable control in recruiting new contributors, but the social environment could be incredibly hostile. Around the time she wrote *The Talnikov Family*, Panaeva began an intimate relationship with Nekrasov. The young poet had pursued her for years, even throwing himself into the Volga River to prove his love. For this (and, one hopes, for other reasons), Panaeva began to return his attentions. Nekrasov moved into the Panaevs' apartment, initiating a ménage-à-trois that would come to emblemize the sexual politics associated with emancipated womanhood in midcentury Russia. Yet, content as the trio was with their arrangement, Panaeva endured a good deal of denigration from the journal's contributors. In a letter to his daughter in 1857, the nobleman writer Ivan Turgenev describes Panaeva as a "rude and nasty woman [*baba*]" who "would certainly drive Nekrasov mad."[3] It's no coincidence that Turgenev describes Panaeva using this dismissive word for peasant women, which was also applied pejoratively to women of other classes. Panaeva's relationship with Nekrasov was often interpreted by their colleagues as a revelation of her true class status, her basic "rudeness." She had spent the first ten years of her marriage gaining the cultural literacy denied to her in youth, and now her relationship with Nekrasov undermined her hard-earned social position in this literary circle.

Still, Panaeva remained committed to this talented collective of writers and critics, influencing the direction of the journal by lobbying for the inclusion of younger writers of mixed-class backgrounds. By the late 1850s, *The Contemporary* had split into two factions: the younger generation of radical writers, including Nikolai Chernyshevsky, Nikolai Dobroliubov, and Fyodor Reshetnikov, and the original, more conservative contributors like Turgenev and Vladimir Sollogub. Panaeva did not claim any political affiliation but, as scholars Jehanne Gheith and Beth Holmgren put it, was "an egalitarian among self-absorbed liberals" and "a pragmatist among self-denying radicals."[4] Gheith argues that Panaeva's tactful mediation between these groups was the crucial, albeit invisible, journalistic labor that underpinned *The Contemporary* in these years.[5] Meanwhile, Panaeva was writing constantly. In 1848, she coauthored a serialized novel with Nekrasov, entitled *Three Countries of the World*. As Panaeva proudly claims in her memoirs, this was the first collaboratively authored novel in Russian literary history. Nekrasov and Panaeva undertook the project together, writing their own chapters and splicing them together, to fill *The Contemporary* during a period when the censor was constantly cutting material right before issues went to print. The critic Vasily Botkin implored Panaev to forbid this coauthorship: "You mustn't shame your journal this way—it's a farce, it degrades literature."[6] But this adventure novel was an instant hit, and fan mail poured into the editorial apartment. While collaborating with Nekrasov to challenge the institution of individual authorship, Panaeva also penned about two dozen novels and works of short fiction independently, including *The Young*

Lady of the Steppes (1855), *Domestic Hell* (1857), and *A Woman's Lot* (1862).[7]

When Ivan Panaev died suddenly in 1862, Panaeva and Nekrasov's relationship ended, and she moved out of the shared apartment. Two years later, she married the critic Apollon Golovachyov and gave birth to a daughter, Evdokia, in 1866. *The Contemporary* closed that year, constrained by an increasingly harsh censorship regime, though Nekrasov and his collaborators continued publishing leftist writings in a journal called *Notes of the Fatherland*. Panaeva's second husband died in 1877. In these years of financial hardship, she wrote what would be her final work, her *Memoirs*. Prized by scholars of nineteenth-century Russian literature for their anecdotal insights into the personal lives of the "great men" of letters, Panaeva's thoughtful and witty appraisals recall the essays of the twentieth-century American writer Eve Babitz, hard at work in Hollywood. Both writers conjure a glittering world of self-obsessed celebrities. They both seem to smirk, but with no pretense of aloofness—after all, they're at the center of these worlds, too. With witty guides like these, who cares whether you're in 1960s Los Angeles or 1860s Saint Petersburg? Panaeva's memoirs appeared in 1889 in the *Historical Herald* to great popularity and were published as a book soon after. A few years later, in March 1893, Avdotya Panaeva died of pneumonia at the age of seventy-four. Her daughter, Evdokia Nagrodskaya, would go on to write *The Wrath of Dionysus*, an internationally bestselling novel that joined Kuzmin, Zinovieva-Annibal, and Teffi in the Russian modernist queer canon, and also served as inspiration for one of the first blockbuster films in Russia. Nagrodskaya fled Russia following the October Revolution, but, ironically, the new regime smiled on her mother's work: it was in 1927, in a critical edition by the critic and poet Korney Chukovsky, that Panaeva's literary debut, *The Talnikov Family*, was published legally, and under her own name, for the first time, eighty years after its original composition.

Back in the 1840s, officially censored but circulated secretly, *The Talnikov Family* enjoyed immediate popularity among the reading public, in no small part because it was in the latest style. Like many of her colleagues at *The Contemporary*, Panaeva rejected the waning aesthetics of Romanticism and instead depicted social life in all its grittiness, embracing a growing interest in so-called "naturalism" in literature. For Panaeva, no detail is too small: the children's ill-fitting clothes, the pies and pâtés meant for guests only, and the incessant squeaking of cockroaches. Panaeva's descriptions epitomize what the literary theorist Viktor Shklovskii would later call "defamiliarization": representing common objects in a way that makes readers feel like they are encountering them for the first time. Natasha enters a churchyard and sees not headstones but "stone dolls." Meeting her tightly corseted governess for the first time, she describes the young woman's purpled shoulders as "cuts of raw beef." Panaeva reminds us that defamiliarization is, among other things, the key mechanism of a good joke. In *The Talnikov Family*, she often uses humor as a handrail when traversing the unsteady grounds of traumatic memory. Panaeva's virtuosic use of defamiliarization indicates that this technique is a fundamental aesthetic tool of the oppressed, a way to estrange the relations of dominance.

To this end, Panaeva often turns her defamiliarizing gaze on the institutions and practices surrounding gender in her time—the governess's raw beef shoulders are just the beginning. Long before puberty, Natasha is a critical observer of gender performance. In a scene emblematic of Panaeva's amused skepticism, Natasha describes the governess performing her toilette before a ball:

> After washing her face, the governess started rubbing it with a red cloth that she dipped in white powder from time to time. She did this with such care that I wondered whether she was trying to do to her face what the floor polishers were doing to the floor. But, to my surprise, her face became covered with a thicker and thicker coat of white. Her eyebrows, eyelashes, freckles—everything disappeared in that cloud of frost, except her evil, brown eyes, peering greedily into the mirror as I stood by holding a candle. The governess guided something over her eye—a distinct eyebrow appeared and her face became lop-sided. But soon everything was set straight: her eyelashes no longer looked like those of someone just come in from the cold. Her lips, smeared with pink lipstick, looked like two red earthworms, and her overworked cheeks were strangely red.

Panaeva's similes drain this ritual of its romance sentence by sentence until the governess becomes a lowly floor polisher, a sort of Archimboldo painting with earthworms for lips. Feminine beauty practices are, in Natasha's eyes, acts of disfiguration—or, at the very least, pretty funny.

In *The Talnikov Family*, Natasha's refusal to perform femininity appears as both a cause and an effect of adults' abuse. Her mother insists that she be punished more harshly because she is "practically a boy." Later, while ill, Natasha reports that, "Like a sexless being, neither a girl nor a boy, and unloved by anyone, I was left to nature." When she's not punished or ignored for her abnormality, Natasha seems to enjoy it: she plays with her brothers, dances the cavalier's part with her sisters, and, when older, abstains from flirting with suitors who bore her. In fact, perhaps because of her relationship to gender, the forms of pleasure available to Natasha are surprisingly diverse for the heroine of a novel about child abuse. She relishes running outdoors, lying in her grandmother's bed listening to stories, and making people laugh with her cheeky impersonations. At the novel's end, during a secret meeting with her fiancé, Natasha is excited about her immanent escape from this repressive domestic setting but also by the surprise of sexual desire felt for the first time.

The Talnikov Family entered raging debates in nineteenth-century Russian society about gender, sexuality, and revolution. Of the many writers in Panaeva's circle, the leftist Chernyshevsky was an especially important interlocutor. His utopian novel *What Is to Be Done?*, written fifteen years after *The Talnikov Family* and published in *The Contemporary*, is closely related to Panaeva's life and fiction. The novel's protagonist, Vera Pavlovna, shares a good deal with Panaeva and her protagonist, Natasha, from physical appearance to key life events. Like Panaeva and Natasha, Vera Pavlovna is brought up in Saint Petersburg by cruel and conniving parents, whom she escapes by marrying a sympathetic young man. However, while Natasha's story ends on the day of her wedding, marriage is only the beginning of Vera's. Chernyshevsky's heroine goes on to organize a women's sewing collective, fall passionately in love, and train to be a doctor. She achieves this through the comradeship of men and women alike. Vera Pavlovna exudes the optimism of a new generation: for her, everything is possible.

In an ironic twist, this character that Panaeva may well have inspired became the standard for female revolutionary sentiment in literature, a standard against which Panaeva's own fiction and politics were unfavorably judged. Unlike Vera Pavlovna and her creator, Panaeva is often very cynical. In her later novels, as Margarita Vaysman and Colleen Lucey illustrate, Panaeva displays a profound skepticism about the reliability of men to promote women's interests. She invests little hope in the emancipatory potentials of love or strategic marriage, key fields of revolutionary change in Chernyshevsky's view.[8] True, *The Talnikov Family* ends with Natasha's love match. But Panaeva's other novels take up the story after marriage, and to call the fates of these heroines bleak would be an understatement.

Yet Panaeva, a true citizen of the nineteenth century, recognizes the imbrication of all the age's "questions": the woman question, the labor question, the serfdom question, and others. For Panaeva, the essential question is always violence, whether against women, the working class, animals, or, indeed, children. In *The Talnikov Family*, Panaeva is preoccupied with the individual's uncanny slide between victimhood and violence. Like other masterpieces in the transnational canon of domestic violence fiction—consider the works of Alice Walker, Gayl Jones,

Alice Munro, Titaua Peu, and Carmen Maria Machado—Panaeva's novel refutes the stable categories of "victim" and "abuser." Instead, violence is like a spirit that takes hold of people and exerts its power over various victims. In the Talnikov household, violence is in the air. Natasha recalls that her father "plunged a fork into the dog's back with the same malicious calm with which he threw a plate at his wife." By the novel's end, readers may be hard-pressed to categorize any character unambiguously as victim or abuser.

And, just as the novel lacks definitive villains, it also lacks a clear hero. Even Panaeva's title suggests this: the novel is not *Natasha* but *The Talnikov Family*. Panaeva's emphasis on the group, constituted more by common space and resources than by biological kinship, suggests a novel about a collective. As Gheith and Holmgren note, Natasha rarely speaks in the first person, but often in the choral "we" of the children, sometimes of all those suffering in the home—which is everyone.[9] And though the novel ends with Natasha's escape through marriage, even this final scene suggests a more complicated story. As Natasha bids goodbye to her siblings and the family dog, we wonder with her: Does it matter that she escapes if everyone else remains trapped? The fantasy of collective liberation is made explicit in *What Is to Be Done?*: after her own marriage, Pavlovna dreams of freeing dozens of girls from their abusive families. Both novels suggest that individual escape is never enough.

To read Panaeva's writing is to recalibrate one's vision until it becomes natural to see collectives where before one saw only individuals. She invites us to imagine: What if *Jane Eyre* was about *all* the children in the school for orphans? And what if, encountering Mr. Rochester's captive wife in the attic, Jane dropped the love plot and joined forces with her? Panaeva's fiction begins to satisfy this yearning for a literature of collective rather than individual liberation. By the same token, Panaeva challenges us to reconsider how we read literature as the product of an individual writer. Whether coauthoring novels or writing her own, Panaeva was embedded in the intellectual and social ecosystem of *The Contemporary*—as were the men whose individual names have come down to us through literary history. In Panaeva's memoirs, these Russian "greats" appear less as independent geniuses and more as a network of people who edited one another, shared tea and wine, wrote letters by turns heartfelt and snarky, and slept together. To celebrate Panaeva is not to add her image to the line of framed portraits displayed in Soviet classrooms: Pushkin, Gogol, Lermontov, Tolstoy, and so on. Instead, to recognize Panaeva is to profoundly reconceive the Russian literary canon itself, to imagine literary history not as a series of portraits but instead as a sort of group portrait.

Part of embracing this portrait is recognizing Panaeva's place among her contemporaries. *The Talnikov Family* is not the sort of even-handed realist novel that would come to characterize Russian prose in the coming decades, the kind of novel that shot writers like Tolstoy and Turgenev to international fame. Readers today may be put off by Panaeva's frequent repetition and non sequiturs. The novel often reads like its author's breathless attempt to recount every impression and every wrongdoing, sometimes at the expense of literary style. Panaeva betrays her position at the tail end of Romanticism: her characters are by turns terrified or delighted, always going pale or turning red.

I preserve these qualities in this translation in order to give readers an accurate sense of Panaeva's style, one developed after Romanticism, during the heyday of the natural school, and on the cusp of realism. However, *The Talnikov Family* also reveals the inherent slipperiness of literary realism: in the violent atmosphere of the Talnikov household, screaming and crying were not melodramatic but, horrifyingly, quotidian. Perhaps the reticence to read this novel as realist is, in fact, a discomfort with the reality of violence.

Near the end of her life, Panaeva wrote that "everyone's character is best discerned in their home environment."[10] *The Talnikov Family* reminds us that, for many people, in the nineteenth century and today, nowhere on earth is more dangerous than the home. But Panaeva's life suggests another way to read this aphorism. Emerging from a childhood much like Natasha's, Panaeva improvised alternative modes of cohabitation and care, building a home that suited her practical yet imaginative character. Dismissing received ideas about what makes a good marriage—and what makes good literature—she built an ephemeral human collective and an enduring literary corpus. My hope is that readers of *The Talnikov Family* will follow its author's lead by taking another look at how we live together and, with equal parts conviction and humor, improvise new kinds of home.

The Talnikov Family

FOUND POSTHUMOUSLY AMONG A WOMAN'S PAPERS

Chapter One

IN A ROOM lit by a dim candle, they washed the dead body of my six-month-old sister. The dull and motionless look in her eyes terrified me. The room was silent; neither my father nor my mother cried. Only the wet nurse cried—about the gilded cap and fur coat that she had lost due to my sister's premature death. If the baby had waited five or six months longer to die, the nurse's work would have been through, and the promised reward would not have slipped through her fingers.

At first, death made a strong impression on me, but given the complete indifference of those around me, and the absence of my father and mother, I concluded that death was not an important thing. The periodic quarrels between my mother and grandmother seemed much more important, judging by my grandmother's copious tears and my mother's terrible screams. My mother would demand an explanation: Where had the housekeeping money gone, and why did our pantry empty out so quickly?

I always took the side of the person crying—whether because I cried a lot myself, I don't know, but I felt sorrier for my crying grandmother than for my angry mother. Every lengthy quarrel was followed by a reconciliation, and Grandmother's fresh tears—no longer sad but joyful—concluded the scene until the next month; that is, until it was time to restock the pantry.

My first memories are from when I was about six years old. We had many relatives living in the house: my mother's two sisters and my father's sister and mother. We loved Grandmother very much because she spoiled us. Mama was little concerned with us, and our father, busy at work, did not pay the slightest attention to his children, whose number increased steadily every year. I already had two sisters, Katya and Sonya, and three brothers, Misha, Fedya, and Vanya.[1] We did not feel much tenderness for our parents, who, for their part, did not show us much affection either. I remember my mother once spent the whole summer taking the waters at the hot springs. On the day she was expected to return, the whole house awaited her, but she didn't come. We were put to bed, but I couldn't sleep—I wanted so badly to see Mama. When everyone had left the nursery, I quietly got out of bed, sat by the window, and started watching the street and listening. But Mama didn't come! I was on the verge of tears, and my heart started beating violently at the slightest noise in the other rooms. At last, the whole house fell asleep, and I did, too, exhausted from waiting. I dreamed that Mama was giving me a big kiss and holding me in her arms—I was so happy. Suddenly I heard noises: Mama was home! I ran downstairs and rushed to her. She seemed surprised at my joy and kissed me. I burst into tears. Everyone surrounded me and asked what was wrong. Why was I crying? I said I was happy to see Mama. They laughed, and Mama, smiling, picked me up. I put my arms around her neck, clung to her tightly, and sobbed harder than ever. She tried to get me to stop, offered me presents, but I refused them and kept crying, covering my face with my hands. My mother decided that I was ill; she said, "Look how she's shaking," and had me taken to the nursery and put to bed. I asked to see her again, but they wouldn't let me.

Our mother rarely showed us affection, rarely bothered with us, but, then again, we rarely felt her wrath; in comparison, the ferocity that occasionally overcame our father was all too tangible. When he lost his temper, he hit anyone who came near him and broke everything he could lay his hands on. Whether he was beating his children or his hunting dog, his face expressed the same desire to quench his rage. He kept the same malicious calm whether he was plunging a fork into the dog's back or throwing a plate at his wife. I remember when my three-year-old brother and I suffered one of his bursts of rage. It was Willow Week, Palm Sunday, and my father returned home from somewhere, ordered breakfast, and drank a whole decanter of vodka. In the corner of our parents' bedroom my brother and I were playing with pussy willows.[2] Father decided to join our game and asked my brother to hit him with one of the branches: "Let's see who hits harder." My brother hit him giddily but in return received such a strong blow that he cried out in pain. My father said, "All right, now it's your turn again. Don't cry! That's the game: whip the willow, tears will follow!" But my brother kept crying, which earned him another blow, followed by several more, slower but no less cruel. Our father was famously strong—he could bend a fireplace poker into a knot. At first, I did not dare to stand up for my brother; as I understood it, parents had the right not only to punish but also to kill their children, and I did not yet understand the concept of injustice. But I forgot everything when I heard my brother's screams: I rushed over and shielded him, leaving my neck and chest exposed to my father. Without noticing, my father started beating me. I kept quiet at first, then screamed—anything to make him stop this cruel game—but, pale and contorted with anger, he continued to hit me evenly and slowly. I don't know when this scene would have ended or what would have happened to us if our mother hadn't come running at the sounds of our screams and dragged our father away. We were covered in blood; my mother, as I recall, pressed me to her heart for the first time in my life. But her tenderness was short-lived; when she came to her senses, she sent me to the nursery and threatened to punish me if I dared to play in her bedroom again without her permission. Father paced the room silently, as if seeking a new object for his rage. Finally, he ordered another decanter of vodka, drank the whole thing, took his hat, and left. The high-pitched squeal of the dog he met in the hallway resounded throughout the house.

Our father usually fell into this mood because of troubles at work, unsuccessful philandering, or his wife's fits of jealousy. I remember once he kissed a pretty woman in front of my mother. I was ready to rush at him when I saw my mother's tears. She made no attempt to conceal her anger. My father left in a rage, taking his guest with him.

Meanwhile, the family was growing every year. Our parents recognized that we needed an education and made us sit at the table with a book for two hours a day. Our lessons consisted of memorizing fables with a moral—"You made your bed, now lie in it"—and some prayers that we couldn't make heads or tails of. This was the extent of our religious upbringing.

We spent a good deal of time trying to determine the identity of the devil, whom we saw at night or in dark rooms, thanks to the absurd stories of our nannies and nurses. We rushed to our aunts with questions about him. They, too, were deprived of life and freedom, and we often bore the consequences; disgruntled with our mother, our aunts took their anger out on us. Their answers to our questions were usually short and emphatic: "Go away! That's enough! I'll box your ears!" And the inquisitive child often returned to the group with red ears and a reinvigorated interest in the debate about the devil.

The only book I ever saw was the alphabet primer, so the nurse's fairy tales were incredibly exciting. If the hero or heroine suffered, we cried and asked the nurse to make them happy, promising her biscuits in return. Biscuits were a form of currency among us. We were each given four biscuits a day, and they were the only property at our complete disposal. I often had to put my dolls up as collateral, however, since I was constantly being punished and left without tea and biscuits. Commerce flourished among us—even personal insults were redeemed with biscuits. Once, irritated by the taunts and various antics of my older sister, who kept me from playing, I was overcome by anger and, oblivious of the consequences, hit her in the face. The injured party ran to the door gleefully and threatened to tell our father, who in such cases severely punished the offender without considering the reasons that compelled such an extreme measure. Certain I could pay my way out, I calmly offered my sister biscuits. But this time, her dignity offended, she rejected the usual recompense and offered me the following condition: I would have to fetch and put away her toys whenever she asked, for a period of five years. I accepted this condition, counting on its absurdity—but I was mistaken. The consequences were unfortunate. For some reason, my pleas and excuses never carried any weight, not only with my elders but also with my brothers and sisters; even the youngest could tear my dolls and dresses and pinch and push me with impunity. I wondered whether it was because I was very dark-complexioned. Then again, my oldest brother was just as swarthy and he did not suffer from it—on the contrary, it gave him some credibility, along with his strength and stubbornness. My sister ordered me around, purposefully ensuring that I was always being torn away from my dolls. One day, my patience finally reached its end, and I refused to obey her orders. She ran to tell our aunt.

My aunt took particular pleasure in punishing me. Her threats rained down on my dark head like hail. But I was not ashamed and flatly declared, "Enough! For three years I've been a fool and obeyed my sister, but from now on I will never fetch her toys again." My ears, my poor ears, were always the first to suffer! My aunt took me by the ear to the corner of the room. I began to cry and complain, but I paid dearly for my resistance: they announced that I was not to eat for a whole week. I was so often left without tea, without dinner, and without supper for a whole month that I was quite accustomed to this sort of punishment. I suffered only when, due to forgetfulness, I would come to the table and they would suddenly shout, "What are you doing here? Did you forget that you're to go without tea today?" Then I would get angry and start crying. Once I was left without cake. My aunt decided to tease me in front of guests and said with a mean smirk, "Give me your plate, I'll serve you some cake!" I blushed all over but immediately recovered and replied that the doctor had forbidden me from eating cake. My aunt's face contorted with rage. She solemnly announced to the guests that I was incorrigible: I had the nerve to joke when I was being punished, and she added that I needed a stronger punishment. After dinner, she fulfilled her promise.

But, apart from these small troubles, until I was ten our life was happy and free. We played all together because our parents did not distinguish between us by gender. Both boys and girls were beaten with birch rods. Only our oldest sister, who was considered a quiet, intelligent, responsible girl, was spared. Sometimes, if I had no troubles of my own, I stood up for the victim and received punishment in their place. But my sister never stirred—she calmly watched her innocent siblings get hurt without shedding a tear.

The death of our grandmother brought the golden days of our childhood to an end. I say "golden" because we would soon lose even those pleasures that we had enjoyed while she was alive. When Grandmother fell ill, she was already sixty years old and couldn't survive a serious illness. One evening her condition worsened considerably; we were all put to bed earlier than usual, which always happened on solemn occasions. Somehow, I had the courage to hide in a dark corner of the room, which was lit by a single icon lamp, and I saw Grandmother's daughter, Aunt Alexandra Semyonovna, sobbing. My mother was also crying, but her tears were nothing like my aunt's and did not move me. My father was serious. Grandmother blessed them all with the icon, said goodbye to them, and asked to see her grandchildren, but my mother said her farewells could be conveyed to them. Grandmother did not insist and, straining her voice, demanded that my mother and father swear before the icon to be kind to the orphan who lay sobbing at her feet. My mother said many things to my dying grandmother, who answered in barely audible sighs and shakes of her head, as if in gratitude—then her head tilted to one side. My father dragged my loudly sobbing mother away from the bed and took her to another room, leaving the nearly dead old woman alone with her daughter by her side. Suddenly afraid, I rushed back to the nursery, where it was quiet and dark, quickly undressed, and went to bed.

In the morning we awoke to a voice repeating "Get up, your grandmother is dead!" I jumped up and ran straight to the room where Grandmother had blessed my parents the night before, but I stopped short at the threshold as if transfixed, numb with horror: on the floor, two women were washing a wrinkled and motionless body, roughly twisting its stiff arms and legs. At first, I could not see the face because it was covered with tangled gray hair, but when one of the women threw the hair back to wash it, I recognized Grandmother. I nearly screamed and ran away. Someone asked me why I was so pale. "I saw Grandmother—some women are washing her!" I answered, trembling. They threatened to punish me for my curiosity but were too busy to follow through. Later, when I saw Grandmother lying on the table in a white cap and hood, I could not understand why I had been so frightened of her that morning.

Almost everyone in our building came to catch a glimpse of Grandmother's insentient face and our weeping aunt. At the coffin, a deacon with a small braid and a nasal voice read something aloud. We entertained him with questions and stories. My mother was openly tender toward my aunt, kissing her incessantly in front of everyone, and sitting beside her and persuading her to eat. I felt very sorry for my aunt. . . . Then came the day of the funeral. We were excited to go to the cemetery, though they had decided to take us only because there was no one to watch us at home. The room where the body lay was filled with people. The mournful singing of the acolytes and my mother's strange screeching made it difficult to breathe, and I also started to cry bitterly. The farewells began. Cold and pensive, our father approached the coffin and kissed his mother, who had very rarely experienced her son's affection while alive. Mama approached next, howling, and paid her last respects to a woman who had suffered many bitter tears and humiliations at her hands. After kissing Grandmother, Mama flailed around, let out a long moan, and finally fell beside the coffin. They dragged her away and began fussing over her. Next was the daughter's turn. Aunt Alexandra Semyonovna was the only person, I think, who loved the deceased and had a right to a farewell kiss. Softly sobbing, she kissed her mother's blue lips, her eyes, and then her lips again—and she would have remained in this position for a long time if my father, her brother, had not torn her from the deceased and handed her over to some bored-looking relatives. Then it was our turn.

Shaking and sobbing from the heavy impression all this had left on me, I kissed Grandmother for the last time. After us came the relatives and strangers with mournful faces, then the servants. Suddenly the room was silent. No one else came up to say farewell, but we all felt some unspoken hesitation to close the coffin. The priest asked, "Has everyone bidden farewell to the deceased?" There was no answer, and he made a sign with his hand. When the lid was placed on the coffin, I felt terribly anguished and suffocated on behalf of Grandmother, as if I were being nailed in with her; the first blow of the hammer shook me so much that I covered my face with my hands and started crying. I don't know how long I cried, but I was roused by my brother, who pushed me and said, "Natasha, run quickly to the carriage—or you'll be left home alone!" Frightened, I ran out after him.

The carriage, leading the slow procession behind the coffin, rocked me into a sweet sleep. When we were let out of the carriage, I ran straight into a field, the first one I had seen in my life. I picked flowers and all sorts of grasses, ran after butterflies, and even caught one, which made me incredibly happy. Then I took pity on the butterfly and gave it the freedom to fly, but the poor thing beat its wings mournfully and moved in circles on my hand; only then did I notice that in my carelessness I had broken one of its wings. I was about to cry when suddenly I heard singing, which reminded me where I was and why I was there. I dropped the butterfly and darted straight toward the singing. Breathless, I joined the procession as we entered a garden with what seemed to me then to be stone dolls. The procession stopped at the open grave. I caught sight of a worm, a very long one, crawling with extraordinary speed along the broken soil. I looked more closely and saw many worms trying desperately to crawl out of the ground, only to disappear into it again just as quickly. Then someone tugged at my dress. I turned around and saw two ugly, wrinkled old women in black headscarves and black cloaks of a strange cut.

"Who are they burying? One of yours?"

"Yes, my grandmother."

"And which one is your mama, the plump one or the skinny one?

"The plump one."

"Oh, it's her, dear thing! How well she wails! So it's her mother who died?"

"No, *that* grandmother is alive."

"So, the poor dear is wailing for someone else's?"

"What do you mean, 'someone else's'? It's my grandmother!"

"So she's the mother of the skinny one?"

"Yes, that's our auntie."

"Who's your father?"

"My father?" I stopped. "Oh, there he is! That's him!"

"No, miss, we want to know what position he holds."

"He's a musician."

"What?" asked one of the old women. "Mu-si-cian?"

She drew out the word. I repeated it: "A musician!"

"Did that granny of yours have any money?" the old woman asked sharply.

I found this sudden change of tone odd. It seemed strange that she had switched to the informal address with me. I answered coldly: "What do you mean?"

"Well, did your granny leave your aunt any money?"

"No!"

I said this to spite the women, not knowing whether my grandmother had money or not.

"Oh, poor woman! An orphan, without a mother or a father!"

Then the two old women began to sigh and sympathize about the orphan's bitter fate. But soon they stopped talking, turning their attention to the bustle of the procession. The coffin was lowered into the grave to the sounds of wailing, crying, and chanting. It was revolting to imagine Grandmother left alone in the ground with all those worms. They started throwing dirt on the coffin. My mother threw her handful rather tragically, then took my aunt by the hand and led her away from the grave, saying: "Come, come, it's all over now!" For the first time my aunt wailed and collapsed onto Mama's chest. I saw this and cried. When my aunt collapsed, I wanted to run to the other side of the grave to get closer to her, but one of the old women grabbed my arm and said, "Why didn't you throw dirt on your grandmother? Look, everyone is doing it!"

"Leave me alone! I don't want to throw worms into my grandmother's grave!"

"Come now! She won't notice a few extra worms!" the other woman chimed in with a vile laugh.

"If you don't throw dirt, then your grandmother will come to you tonight in a shroud and . . ."

Without listening to the rest of the old woman's terrible words, I threw flowers into the grave, broke free from her grasp, and ran after my mother. The old women's laughter followed me like the cawing of crows.

Once I reached the church, I was immediately squeezed into a carriage filled with my brothers and sisters. Our mother asked the girl who was watching us, "Is everyone here?" and she replied, "Yes, ma'am," and then she counted us with her finger: eight in all, that is, no more or less than our total number. We set off, but after a few yards, the carriage had to stop. A small coffin was being carried toward us; a pale woman was stumbling after it, overcome. She wrung her hands and wailed, as if she wanted to stop the procession. It was the first time I had seen such deep despair, and I was very surprised that a person could cry so bitterly about a small child. I remembered the death of my sister, for whom no one cried. Mama hastened to relieve my confusion. "What a fool! What is she crying about?" she said as the sobbing woman passed. "A real treasure she's lost. Must be her first! I've got plenty to spare!" Then she poked her head out of the carriage and angrily shouted to our coachman, "Hey halfwit, what are you waiting for?" The coachman started at this unexpected address, and his fright dispersed as if by electric shock along the bony sides of the horses, who, starting in turn, successfully moved forward after two or three desperate attempts. The journey seemed very short to me; we each shared our impressions and spoke of our adventures around the cemetery. Some spoke of worms, others of the dead—of whom there were many that day.

We arrived home. The rooms had been completely transformed. Instead of a coffin, I saw a long table loaded with various bottles. There were many guests; soon everyone took their seats, except for the children, who had no seats because the deacons were at our table. The meal was served.

The silence was terrible, so I peeked in from the other room to see whether they were waiting to nail Grandmother's coffin closed again. But I was reassured—instead of a coffin, I saw the guests' satisfied faces; instead of incense, I smelled fish soup and a huge salmon pie. They ate a lot and for a long time. I grew tired of watching people chew and chew, and the slow rocking of their dazed heads filled me with gloom.

Despite those three days of terror, I enjoyed the funeral. For the first and last time in my childhood I felt free, probably because no one was thinking about my existence.

Chapter Two

MAMA'S SYMPATHY soon ran dry: that evening she parted coldly from Aunt Alexandra Semyonovna and, in the morning, got angry with her for the mess in the kitchen and the nursery. Before six weeks had passed, our aunt asked for her inheritance, which consisted of an icon, an old coat, and two down pillows. Instead of tenderness and concern, Mama offered our aunt unlimited power in the nursery and limited control in the kitchen.

Before long there were big changes. Our mother decided that the presence of children in the drawing room or her bedroom was superfluous, and we were strictly forbidden from entering those areas. Even our decade-long custom was abolished: we no longer kissed our parents' hands. "Children are bothersome enough throughout the day, even without that," our mother said, "and my health does not allow me to trouble with them!" Perhaps to improve her poor health, she spent not only all day but also all night playing cards. We were frightened to approach her at times; a sleepless night or a significant loss at cards irritated her so much that she often canceled the morning hand-kissing herself, fearing the consequences. Our father was displeased with his wife's passion for cards. Frequent quarrels over money turned Mama more and more bitter against the children. To calm her conscience, she even began to keep accounts, which clearly indicated to our father that her passion for cards cost some hundreds a year, while the children were costing them thousands. In fact, it was the opposite. The morning was an especially onerous time for everyone in the house. The cook was scolded for failing to work a miracle: feeding twenty-five people with what was barely enough for ten. Our aunt was blamed for everything: the maid's errors, the guests' liberal consumption of wine, and the children, whom our mother had not laid eyes on all day. In short, our mother shouted and punished people not in response to their behavior but according to her losses in cards. By some trick of fate, I always found myself first on the receiving end of her irritation. Once, noticing me in the mirror as my aunt was combing her hair, my mother demanded that I read aloud. I began reading; for every mistake she gave me a shove against my head or my back. Tears prevented me from reading, and I made mistakes on every word. In a rage, she finally hit me so hard on the hand I was using to trace the words that the book flew into the air and my hand cracked and collapsed like a weight. I yelped and blanched from the pain.

My father was clearly delighted by his wife's vehemence: he himself had been barred from housekeeping and childrearing on account of his short temper, and now he had an opportunity to reproach his wife, whose passion for cards had produced similar consequences. He examined and stretched my hand while I sobbed. At last, he ordered me to the nursery. I went, thus freed from reading, but the pain did not prevent me from hearing my parents' conversation as I left:

"You think she doesn't need to learn to read?"

"What's the point in teaching her to read when she has nothing to write with?"

Then my mother began speaking very quickly, and by the time I reached the nursery, their conversation had devolved into screams and tears.

Our fate was sealed: they decided to hire a governess. Unfortunately, it wasn't long before a candidate appeared. A lady we knew fired her governess for excessive harshness toward the children. Despite the terrible constraint of her corset, to which she subjected herself voluntarily and with exemplary self-sacrifice, this twenty-four-year-old, who said she was twenty-one, loved having complete freedom in her dealings with children. The poor things' ears were always covered in blood. This governess purposely grew out the nail of her middle finger and cut it in a point, so that even her "harmless" punishments would be felt more intensely. When her corset prevented her from raising her arm high, she ordered her victim to kneel, pulled them up by the ear or hair, and told them to squat down. Disobedience was met with more punishment. She held up a ruler and stated her conditions in advance: "If you put out your palm nicely, you'll get ten, but if you try anything, you'll get twenty."

The governess's exemplary strictness and corresponding educational philosophy decided the matter very quickly: she was hired for four hundred rubles a year in cash to teach whatever she wanted, to handle morality however she pleased, and to punish as much and by whatever means suited her. She was even given the right, if it proved necessary, to request the footman's assistance when punishing our brothers, who were quite strong. Before being presented to the governess, we were washed, combed, and dressed up. I was introduced as a "person of interest" who required vigilant supervision and particular strictness.

"She's practically a boy, even plays with them. And how lazy she is! She bursts into tears at the mere sight of a book!"

The governess assured my mother that there was hope for my correction, saying to me, "Mademoiselle Nathalie, you must behave yourself. Otherwise, I will punish you like the boys."

The governess's physiognomy was not pleasing to any of us in the least. Her red hair was arranged with extraordinary care. Her mean, brown eyes quickly darted around and then stopped on their object, as if seeking to penetrate it. Her huge mouth was constantly smiling, which gave her large round face—always red and covered with countless freckles and white powder—an evil and cloying look. Her waist defied all probability: it was so drawn in that her rather fat and wide shoulders, covered with brown freckles, were completely purple and resembled cuts of raw beef.

The governess's clothes were as unpleasant as she was. Her soft, white hands were disfigured by her blue nails and countless rings, whose emeralds and rubies, according to one of our aunts' careful investigations, were, in fact, fake. But this discovery did not in the least interfere with their friendship; in exchanging various secrets and favors relating to their toilettes with the governess, our aunts found that their hostile feelings toward the

French language (on which our governess was the household authority) were for a time completely extinguished. We noticed that our aunts' faces had lately turned white as well.

As for us, the first order of business was that we transform from Sonya, Katya, and Natasha into Sophie, Catherine, and Nathalie. Our brothers became Jean, Michel, and so on. The governess called each of our aunts "*ma chère*" and they started doing the same to her.

"*Ma chère*, Catherine must be punished."

"Very well, *ma chère*, I will not give her the sweets she was promised today."

The punishments were calculated so that our aunts and the governess received double portions of cake or dessert. We were ordered to call the governess *Mademoiselle*. We made swift progress in French: *permettez-moi sortir, pardonnez-moi*. I learned the latter very quickly.[1]

Our freedom was restricted even further. We children were all confined to one room. The room adjacent to it was turned into a combination schoolroom, sewing room, dining room, and the bedroom shared by our three aunts and the governess. (I should mention that we, along with our aunts, stopped eating at the main table after the death of our grandmother.) We were forbidden from entering the room after school hours. The room to which they confined us was too small for eight children, though this fact did not prevent them from building an entresol, where they kept the entire household's dirty linens, all sorts of junk, and the children's wardrobe, hardly luxurious. But then, so many cockroaches took up residence in this room that it was never completely silent. Whenever we quieted down, there was a dull, mysterious rustle that sounded like the poetic fluttering of leaves shaken by the wind. Woe to anyone who left anything edible there: everything was immediately devoured by the ravenous insects. As soon as a baby was born, the nurse settled in with it on the entresol, in the company of a laundress who was in the habit of getting dead drunk. Our mother would not see the child for six weeks, claiming that a change of air would be harmful for the baby and that her own health did not allow her to climb the stairs. She especially disliked her daughters. Her reasoning went along these lines:

"As soon as a boy grows up, he's out of sight. But you've got to keep girls around until they get married, and who's going to marry them? Their father is broke, and no one's lining up to look at their faces. . . . How did we end up with children like these? Their father isn't bad looking, and their mother . . ." Here she would stop, giving whatever woman who had come to her for help a chance to speak. And when that woman responded, "Marya Petrovna, ma'am, you are a princess! If your daughters take after you, they'll have to beat the suitors off with sticks, even without dowries." Then my mother would conclude, "Yes, well, what can I say, God's rewarded us with freaks. If you only knew how ugly their feet are. . . . Dreadful! Mine, at least, are . . ."

It should be noted that her own feet were incredibly large and ugly and so, when talking about someone, she usually began with their feet, attacking them with excessive ferocity, especially if they weren't bad. Then she worked her way up to the person's head. My mother was quite thorough. She went over her daughters' shortcomings with such pleasure and delight, the same way a tender, loving mother talks about her children's merits without omitting even the most insignificant, even inventing good qualities in her excessive fervor.

Whenever the nurse went downstairs, she was reprimanded for bustling around the entire house and then forbidden from going downstairs without being called for. It goes without saying that in this state of affairs, sick children were cared for very poorly.

Once on a winter evening we were sitting on the entresol by the light of a candle floating in a jar of vegetable oil. The groans of our sick brother, mixed with the sleeping laundress's ravings, forced us to stop fooling around and discuss the situation.

"What if he dies? It'll be scary to sit on the entresol!"

We were startled by a strange cry from the bed in the corner. We glanced back and saw the trembling laundress rising, her short hair disheveled and face pale. Terrified, we called out to her. She jumped up and rushed at us, shouting, "Go away, you devils! You'll be the death of me!"

We ran out shrieking, knocked over the night-light, and didn't so much run as roll down the stairs. The nanny and the nurse came running at our cries and, after questioning us, went to the entresol. Everything was upside-down: the bench overturned, pillows and coats on the floor. My brother was convulsing terribly in his cradle. After five minutes, his suffering ended. The poor child had probably been scared.

Our mother was playing cards at the time. To everyone's surprise, when she was informed of her son's death, she began to scream and cry. The child was ordered buried as soon as possible because the sight of a dead child pains a mother's heart even more than its suffering. She retreated to her room, screaming, but not for long. The next day, in the evening, the child was buried very simply and quietly. If tears were shed over him, they were only the tears of siblings quarreling nearby and hitting each other over some toy. Funerals usually went like this: a carriage was hired, then people came to ask my parents whether they would like to say goodbye to the body. My mother endured these difficult moments with an amazing calm that did credit to her strength. The whole scene ended very quickly. She went up to the coffin, made the sign of the cross over the child, and casually kissed him on the forehead, saying, "God be with him! No need to cry—there are plenty left!" However, she needn't have uttered comforting words at all because the faces of those present clearly expressed a reserve of courage sufficient to endure such a loss. Our father, who did not enjoy sitting at home, was not always present for the removal of the body.

In this way, three of my sisters and one brother were buried.

Chapter Three

THE GOVERNESS quickly settled on an educational program that completely fulfilled our parents' requirements and thereby earned their full favor. From the moment she took us on, children's laughter died out in the house. Our constant tears proved that the woman to whom we had been entrusted was tirelessly devoted to our moral education and our parents' peace. Our governess had a well-developed oppressor's spirit. Perhaps she wanted to recreate the system of tyranny in which she herself had been brought up. If so, those seeds had indeed not fallen on barren soil. No prank escaped her hawklike eyes; she sought each criminal with incredible persistence, and if she failed to discover them by various signs or interrogations, she submitted to the will of fate and punished the innocent along with the guilty. Sometimes, intimidated by her threats and shoves, my younger brothers betrayed the older ones. The governess relished this. But sometimes she was unable to remain at the heights of decency until the conclusion of the case. Having announced her verdict with dignity, she sometimes stooped to the role of executioner herself. Then she would morph from executioner into spy, occasionally enduring humiliations in this role. Noticing her approach from the entresol, we tried to bait her with our conversations:

"What happens to eavesdroppers in the next world?"

"They roast them slowly on a fire."

"No, they use the breaking wheel."

"They rip out their veins!"

And then we poured water on the governess's head and let loose a cloud of fluff from a torn pillow. When we succeeded, of course, we burst out laughing and gave ourselves away. Shame prevented the governess from immediately punishing us, but on occasion we paid dearly for our momentary triumphs. The older girls, however, were not subjected to rods. And my brother Misha often escaped punishment because he was brave and strong. If the governess managed to punish him, he took every possible revenge on her and our aunts, to our indescribable joy. He was rude to them, even laughed at them, so that at last, frightened, they began to avoid quarreling with him. My other brothers and I suffered on everyone's behalf. We were sub-jected to all sorts of punishments, indiscriminately and without bounds. Sunday was a day of massacre in our house. The inno-cent were punished in anticipation of their future crimes.

After reading our prayers, at nine o'clock in the morning we sat down to our lessons; at one o'clock we finished and were brought breakfast, which I almost never got to taste. I loved doing impressions of people, and I was so good at it that, to my surprise, people immediately guessed who I was imitating. Sometimes the governess, who liked to prove her diligence by the number of children she punished, would suddenly turn to me and inform me that I would be left without breakfast that day. To console myself I quietly replied, "I didn't even want breakfast," but after returning to the entresol, I stuffed myself with kvass, bread, and salt, afraid that I would also be denied dinner. And my fear often proved well-founded.

After dinner, at about four o'clock, we returned to our lessons. We were not allowed to study during class. We took dictation and most often read from the Bible. One person read aloud and the others listened. Sometimes, the governess unexpectedly ordered another person to continue, and the slightest confusion on our part provoked severe punishment. The offender had to kneel for the rest of class, which lasted until seven o'clock. The governess herself found the length of class burdensome because even the most brilliant teacher finds it hard to occupy children for ten hours a day. But Mama, having placed us at the governess's complete disposal, strictly demanded one thing of the governess in return for unlimited power: constant supervision of the children. Mama resolutely barred the governess from leaving the property on weekdays. Our aunts guarded her like two dragons. If the governess finished lessons ten minutes early, they would reprimand her and threaten to tell Mama.

The governess loved men in uniform with an uncontrollable passion. She would rush to the window whenever she heard a regimental march or glimpsed an officer's epaulets. Sometimes an officer would wave at her, probably not suspecting that she was the teacher of so many children, and she would return to the table all red and for a long time ignore all the disturbances that had arisen in her absence. But our aunts, who were always sitting in the same room and quietly spying on us, immediately told the governess everything we had done, sarcastically hinting at her weakness for officers. Hints turned into barbs, and mutual reproaches rained down like hail: about rouge, coquetry, marriage plans, secret thoughts, and innocent tricks—nothing was forgotten in those moments. Their cries were frightening: everyone spoke all at once and their movements were sharp and strange. We stopped reading and listened with strained attention. To our great annoyance, Aunt Alexandra Semyonovna would appear and separate the heated young ladies. But from time to time, they would shoot each other angry glances and exchange curses, like flames suddenly bursting out of the blackened mass after a fire, illuminating the terrible destruction for a moment, and then vanishing. Everything was covered in darkness again until a new flame flashed up somewhere else.

On those days we could be naughty and rude to our aunts with impunity—the governess even encouraged us. However, they reconciled quickly and simply without any explanations or apologies. They knew they didn't have any score to settle and, bored by silent sulking, returned to their favorite conversations, secrets, and plans, putting their united efforts toward persecuting the children.

Aunt Alexandra Semyonovna, who was busy with the household, did not have time to participate in her nieces' and nephews' punishment. And she probably did not want to: she was kind and seemed to love us. But our mother's sisters could not help but feel embittered toward her children. Their life—sedentary, confined to one room, monotonous, with constant sewing and incessant gossip—could embitter even the most mild-tempered of spinsters, and our aunts were already over twenty-five. The hope of marriage warmed their hearts less and less each day. To be fair, men visited our nursery, by virtue of past acquaintance, but they were so poor and pathetic that even our aunts did not dare count on them. The only exception was a young man named Kirilo Kirilych. Tall, thin, with a long nose, red face, eyes like a rabbit (but without its simple-minded expression), and long, blond hair, he was not particularly handsome, but what he lacked in beauty he more than made up for in dexterity, courtesy, and a good fortune. Our aunts' hearts, easily inflamed to begin with, began to burn. Even Mama paid Kirilo Kirilych special attention, which she did not bother hiding from her sisters or the governess or, consequently, from us. From our entresol we watched our aunts' and governess's coquetry and eavesdropped on their friendly conversations, in which we played an important role. How? We found a small crack in the wall above the stove, close to the ceiling. Little by little I made a hole, like a dormer window. Climbing into the gap between the stove and the ceiling, I not only listened but also saw everything that our enemies were doing in the other room. We enjoyed this invention for quite a while, sometimes using expressions that we overheard from our aunts. On those occasions, they would quickly exchange glances as if to ask, "Where did they learn that?" In the end, however, our observation point was closed—and in a very unfortunate way.

Once, settling into my spot above the stove, I accidentally sent up some dust, which treacherously rushed into my throat and nose, as if trying to avenge the violation of its calm rest. I braced myself and closed my eyes but, to my horror, let out a great sneeze. The chatter died down below. I still could have saved myself, but unfortunately the first sneeze wasn't the last: I sneezed again and again, and when at last I managed to free half of my body from the observation point, I couldn't save the other half. The governess set upon me, attacking my ears like a bulldog. I found myself in the nursery, surrounded by a furious chorus of scolding aunts. When the first outburst of indignation had passed, the governess made me kneel and ordered me to go without both tea and supper, even though I had been denied dinner that day and was very much counting on supper. I was also forbidden from going to sleep; I was made to kneel until two o'clock in the morning. Finally, the governess let me go to bed, promising a new punishment the next day. I rose from my knees in excruciating pain and forced myself to walk to the nursery. It was silent—my brothers and sisters were fast asleep. I was in so much pain that my sobs woke up my brother Ivan. He took a piece of bread from under his pillow, quietly put it in my hand and said, "Eat quick, Natasha! The redhead might search us again!"

"How did you hide it, Vanya?"

"I put it in my boot. The witch came to search us, to see if we'd hidden something for you. But we fooled her. She sniffed around, said it smelled like bread, only where could it be? Couldn't find it."

"She really couldn't find it?"

"No, I cheated the damned woman! She dug through the whole bed, told me to get up. Then Misha gave her a good push, as if in his sleep. 'Strange,' he said, 'I must have been startled, I myself don't remember what I did.'"

"They're going to punish me again tomorrow." And I started crying.

"Don't cry, Natasha! She'll forget by then."

After offering me consolation (which he didn't believe in the least), my brother fell back asleep. I was not so fortunate and, after finishing the bread soaked with my tears, I could not sleep for a very long time. When I did fall asleep, I dreamed that I was enduring the day's punishments all over again.

As time went on, Kirilo Kirilych gained more and more clout in our household. Mama's toilette underwent a striking change. She combed her hair much more carefully, and once a week she voluntarily subjected herself to torture: pulling out the gray hairs that were barely beginning to show. Her face started to look amazingly fresh, thanks to a plant that subsequently revolution-ized sugar production.[1] Her waist, which had enjoyed freedom for fourteen years, was suddenly encased in a corset. Dressing gowns were replaced by dresses. An embroidery frame appeared in the drawing room, even though she had never embroidered in her life. At first glance, she could seem attractive: tall, moderately plump, which is appealing in women of a certain age. She had a small face, a straight nose, a rather good mouth (while it was closed), unusually white and even teeth, and finally—a rarity in women, even beauties—a beautifully shaped neck, one that could rival Mary Stuart's.[2] In short, she was not a bad-looking woman. Only her eyes disturbed the harmony of her face: small, dull, and harsh, they darted around quickly and never seemed to smile, as if they were made only for anger. However, this defect was apparently not too striking because she was generally thought to be a very beautiful woman, which she took great confidence in. Her brand of coquetry clearly revealed her rude nature and lack of education—it consisted of unpleasant and often inappropriate laughter, mouth contortions, and sharp movements.

For some time, everything in the house was subject to Kirilo Kirilych. Dinner, tea, even cards—everything depended on his taste and disposition. Mama began to order dinner herself, saying, "Sashenka, order such and such dish. Andrei"—her husband, that is—"is very fond of it. . . . And for the children you can warm up something from yesterday." Very often my father dined separately and much earlier, depending on his work or his hunting and billiards. Like a complete stranger in the house, he didn't notice anything around him and raised his voice only at dinner when he thought a dish was bad. He only entered our nursery to see the five cages of birds he had installed in our room. And when you saw the way he cared for his larks, warblers, canaries, and bullfinches, it was impossible not to recognize in him a loving and tender heart. How carefully he investigated every cage— whether it was cleaned, whether there was food and water. How angry he became over the slightest carelessness shown by my sister, Katya, to whom he entrusted his fledglings' physical needs. And with what exemplary patience he himself developed the birds' mental strength and talents, whistling for two hours on end like a finch or tapping a knife on a plate to encourage a lark! Joy would shine in his eyes when the lark finally burst into a shrill cry, as if suddenly appreciating the inexhaustible affection of its benefactor and deciding to reward him generously. With the untiring tenderness of the head of a large family, our father cleaned his larks' feet. When he noticed that one of his dogs, also in our care, was sluggish, he gave it a ball of sulfur and the next morning demanded a report from us: Is the dog better? No wonder he had no time left for anything else! Sometimes he would interrupt our studies and order us to catch flies and cockroaches. Our nursery went totally silent other than occasional joyful exclamations: "Oh, what a fat one!" "Oh, what a black one!" Our father, who was sitting at the table impatiently waiting to give the birds a treat, finally said, "That's enough!" We approached him with our offerings as if he were some Indian deity. We tore off the legs, wings, and antennae of our victims, who were buzzing sadly, and put them on the table. Fearing for his birds' health, our father became very angry when he noticed a fly with a thread tied to it or a cockroach covered in red sealing wax. And there were quite a few of these. Lacking toys, we would sometimes tie a long string to a fly's legs and follow its flight. It flew tirelessly, frightening other flies and amusing us during our long lessons. And how afraid we were whenever one of those flies, with its long tail, came out of nowhere, buzzing around the room and landing on the head of our sullen and anxious father. What if he noticed? The cockroaches were a different story. We would cut a horse out of playing cards and glue a cockroach under each of the horse's legs with sealing wax. We did the same thing with paper geese and ducks, and often a whole flock of these never-before-seen animals ran with extraordinary speed to the crevices of the room as we screamed with joy.

My brothers didn't have companions, and my sisters and I had no real friends. I remember only one close acquaintance: the daughter of a laundress who started working for us to replace the other one, who drank. Her name was Ulyana but we called her Ulya. She darned our brothers' stockings and washed our aunts' handkerchiefs. I often helped her so that she could finish sooner and come play dolls with us. She taught us lots of songs. Together we sang, "Little bunny rabbit, where have you been? Out, miss, out, miss, Running through the glen!"

Once, Ulya returned from the shop out of breath and told us that the coachman had put his arms around her. I told her she ought to hit rude men like that.

"Come now, miss! People like him are strong, after all!"

"Well, then, grab some tobacco and throw it in his eyes!" I instructed Ulya passionately.

She told us about her adventures: once, when she worked as a nanny, a civil servant offered her a jar of lipstick, two pairs of cotton stockings, and a pair of two-kopeck coins.

"Oh, Ulya, what a fool you are! Why didn't you take it? You could have bought yourself two dolls!"

"Yes, miss, but what about my mama?"

"She wouldn't have found out."

"No, miss, she would've! He kept asking me to kiss him, and if you kiss a man, the trouble is, everyone will find out!"

"What do you mean? I saw how many times Luka kissed you, and nothing . . ."

"You don't understand what I mean, miss!" Ulya said mysteriously.

"Oh, Ulya, darling, tell us!"

And we moved closer to Ulya. With great seriousness she told us how one of her friends had accepted a gift from someone and how her mother had beaten her and thrown her out.

"But how did her mother find out, Ulya?"

Ulya smiled.

"Oh, how stupid you young ladies are!"

Mama began to visit the nursery in the evenings to see Kirilo Kirilych, who sometimes came to chat with our aunts. When he joked with them, Mama was cross. When he joked with her, they were cross. In short, there was never a moment of peace. Mama's visits hardly improved our situation: the governess immediately put us to bed so that we wouldn't disturb her. If it was still very early, she put us in the corners of the room, and the nursery came to resemble a family crypt decorated with statues. Mama hardly noticed the sepulchral silence of the room, and only when we unintentionally burst into laughter did she ask, surprised, "Aren't the children asleep?"

"Not yet," the governess answered proudly. "They have been punished today."

When she chanced to pay attention, Mama was surprised to see that her children were growing up just like any others. In fact, our many battles made us even stronger, and we were growing well.

Our sister Sofia was turning out to be the prettiest and, despite efforts to make her remain a child, began to attract the attention of men. She was fourteen years old and her waist did not yet know the touch of a corset, which perhaps contributed to her rapid development. A dress that was always too short and too tight, bloomers that sometimes stuck out from under her dress (a fashion inspired, I believe, by naval pantaloons), and a tiny pelerine that barely covered her magnificent shoulders—such was my sister's attire. Her abundant hair, combed into two braids, reached down to her knees. Her face was unusually fresh and her eyes unusually attractive. Once, when I was holding wool for my mother in the drawing room, a poor lady visited and asked Mama to serve as godmother to her daughter, announcing that Kirilo Kirilych had promised to be her godfather. When she saw Sofia passing through the room, she said, "Well, Marya Petrovna! How your Sofia Andreevna has grown, and gotten pretty, too! There's a bride for you!"

Mama's face changed, and, after examining her daughter closely from head to toe, she said passionately, "Yes, their mother and father work themselves to the bone, and these children just get fatter!"

"Well, Marya Petrovna, you won't have to trouble yourself over her much longer. I think you already have some nice little suitors in mind for Sofia Andreevna. Wouldn't Kirilo Kirilych make a fine match? Heaven knows, he's well able to feed a wife and children."

A blow to the forehead, accompanied by the words "Look, you're dropping it!" drew me out of the intentness with which I had been listening to the conversation. I involuntarily lowered my hands and then the skein became truly tangled. Mama untangled it very carefully.

I told my sisters everything, but we didn't spend much time making fun of Sofia, calling her Kirilo Kirilych's bride. Pleading poor health, Mama sent Sofia to the christening in her place.

In winter we never had any exercise, and if we hadn't snuck out to the yard, where, as if we'd broken free from our chains, we jumped around, rolled in the snow, and did somersaults, then we might have suffocated from the bad air in the nursery. But during the summer holidays, when the governess was relaxing after all the hard work of educating us, we enjoyed complete freedom for two months. We were given a ticket to the public gardens and left there every morning without any supervision. Even when it rained and stormed, they did not come for us before the usual time. My brothers terrorized everyone, climbing trees and gazebos and breaking everything they touched. I almost always took part in their games, usually pretending to be kidnapped by robbers (that is, my brothers). The other boys there played Cossacks and, sometimes, all riled up, they began to fight with the robbers in earnest.[3] Then the hostage tried to separate them, but nothing could convince them to stop. Like roosters, as soon as they caught their breath, they were at each other again. Only exhaustion put an end to the fighting.

Those two months passed in a flash. The governess returned, stricter than ever, and the stuffiness and constant agony resumed until the next summer. But even those rare intervals of freedom and happiness soon ended. After three years, the gardens were closed and after that we didn't play outside in the summer.

One winter, Kirilo Kirilych got it in his head to dance, and our nursery was transformed into a ballroom. Our aunts jumped around, as did my sisters Katya and Sonya. The governess waltzed very deftly, with the grace of an educated young lady. They left me out because I was too little. In my vexation, I started dancing alone in another room. At last, I learned everything that my aunts and sisters knew, and even managed to imitate everyone, including Kirilo Kirilych himself, who was an unrivaled dancer. Once they were short one man and wanted to teach me how to fill in, but I proudly showed them that

I already knew how; I impersonated the absent cavalier so successfully that I was forced to reprise the role several times.

At Kirilo Kirilych's request, Mama promised to throw a ball at Christmastime. Christmas came, the governess went home to her mother, and we could all breathe more easily. Our aunts told fortunes every night, but a husband still wouldn't emerge for Stepanida Petrovna.[4] Once she ran outside and asked the first passerby, "What's your name?" to find out the name of her future husband. "Matryona!" called a woman's voice in reply. Stepanida Petrovna was very angry and started carefully putting a black cockroach in a pill box under her pillow every single night, and in the morning, there would be endless accounts of her dreams.

At last, the day of the ball came: it was New Year's Eve. We were excited to see people dressed up and dancing but, to our horror, that morning the governess appeared, curlers in her hair, and immediately managed to deprive someone of tea and sweets. The whole house was in an uproar. Mama raged and shouted. Aunt Alexandra Semyonovna, like Figaro, was trying to be everywhere at once.[5] The floor polishers came, and our cries and laughter were accompanied by squeaking and shuffling. We were dressed—very poorly. Everything was short and tight on us. Our sisters' hair was braided, much to the chagrin of our aunts and the governess, and only Alexandra Semyonovna's persistent intercession with our mother saved the girls' hairstyles. Mama was completely dressed up. The governess quarreled with Aunt Stepanida Petrovna over me—each wanted me to dress her. I laced up corsets and dresses more deftly than anyone else in the house—I was the only one strong enough.

But the governess resolutely announced that, as my educator, she would not let me go until she herself had dressed. And so began her toilette. After washing her face, the governess started rubbing it with a red cloth that she dipped in white powder from time to time. She did this with such care that I wondered whether she was trying to do to her face what the floor polishers were doing to the floor. But, to my surprise, her face became covered with a thicker and thicker coat of white. Her eyebrows, eyelashes, freckles—everything disappeared in that cloud of frost, except her evil, brown eyes, peering greedily into the mirror as I stood by holding a candle. The governess guided something over her eye, and a distinct eyebrow appeared and her face became lopsided. But soon everything was set straight: her eyelashes no longer looked like those of someone just come in from the cold. Her lips, smeared with pink lipstick, looked like two red earthworms, and her overworked cheeks were strangely red. She moved on to her hair: those thin strands squeaked pitifully at the touch of the red-hot tongs. Curls were removed and each clump of hair, fluffed to an incredible degree, formed its own ringlet, and the governess started looking like a red-haired lapdog. Then she took a thick braid out of the dresser and gave it to me to hold while she oiled, straightened, and brushed it. Then she skillfully attached it to her own skinny braid, pinning it with an incredible number of pins, making her head look for a moment like a fence studded with nails to fend off thieves. Finally, having arranged everything properly, the governess smiled, pleased with her luxurious coiffure. While she was gazing intently at her own face in the mirror, which flattered her with the same attentions, I diligently laced her corset with new red cording, which had been taken from a bunch of quill feathers (no other cords could withstand the ordeal, often weakening and bursting at the most critical moment). The governess reluctantly left the mirror—she seemed truly enchanted by the face that stared at her with endless ecstasy. The tightening began: I pulled at her with incredible zeal, nearly breaking her in half. Her face and neck, despite the entire box of powder spent on them, turned crimson. After putting on countless skirts, the governess donned a white muslin dress so low cut that, were it not for the lace shoulder straps, its front would certainly not have held up. But the straps, digging into her plumpness, completely disappeared into her shoulders: such was the force of this precautionary measure inspired by modesty! After finishing her toilette, the governess released me to Aunt Stepanida Petrovna and began adorning herself with various earrings, signets, and rings. My mother's sisters, upon seeing the governess, were so enraged that they took her outfit as a personal insult and shouted in a tone of confused innocence, "*Ma chère*, we will be embarrassed for you!"

Advice and entreaties to wear a wrap poured forth like a river, but the governess only felt more confident in the invincible charm of her outfit: she knew these jealous aunts. . . . Our aunts' toilettes resembled that of the governess, only they did not attach anything to their braids, since they had their own. They began bustling more and more, sewing their bodices in such a way that even the governess's modesty would be offended.

Their toilette likely would have lasted much longer if a chord of music had not announced that it was time. Everyone fussed and groaned; the governess threw a farewell glance at her worried face in the mirror and, after gathering us all, prepared to enter the hall. Our aunts brushed the red cloth over their faces once more, causing a bright blush to rise on their cheeks, and joined us. We entered the brightly lit hall. Many guests had already arrived. When our aunts saw Mama superbly dressed up, they winked and shrugged, probably pitying their older sister's self-delusion. The dancing began. As if to spite our aunts and the governess, we were constantly engaged—I even danced a quadrille with an adjutant. I was sitting with Stepanida Petrovna when he approached me, and she did not doubt that the invitation was for her. She immediately began to pull on her gloves and even rose halfway from her chair but, trembling, collapsed back onto it. I hurriedly gave my hand to my beau. During the dance I stood directly across from my aunt, who was sitting on pins and needles and throwing threatening glances around. At the same time, as if to spite my mother, Kirilo Kirilych was currying favor and dancing with my sisters. Mama grew angry and even said, "Isn't it time for the children to go to bed? They're only getting in the way."

Our aunts and the governess had been waiting for this moment. They immediately ordered us to the nursery. We nearly cried, and the governess, probably afraid we might try to return to the hall, personally oversaw our undressing. After confiscating our shoes and our brothers' boots, she locked all the footwear in her dresser. What a terrible predicament we were in! The talk, shuffling, and music not only kept us awake but also tormented us. When we heard the screeching and laughter of the masked dancers, we all jumped out of our beds at once, as if on command, and rushed to the doors of the hall. The older ones took the best spots and the younger ones found others, some perching above their older siblings with the help of a chair, others crouching and taking shelter at their feet. We all fixed our eyes on the crack that revealed a bright strip of light. Then. . . . Oh, the horror! Fascinated by the spectacle, one of us leaned heavily on the door. It opened with a creak, and we tumbled out into the hall, along with the chairs. Only our eldest sister managed to hide. The guests rushed to us, but our pain was eclipsed by fear, and we immediately ran away and rushed to our beds, our hearts beating violently. Our speedy escape did not save us. The chairs, scattered like ruins in the doorway, testified to our flourishing presence. The governess didn't even need to question us. She ordered us out of bed. We got up, and, after she scolded us and promised to take away our tea, dinner, and supper the next day, she sent everyone to the corners. Then, locking the door to the hall, the governess went back to indulge in a delightful waltz.

This punishment deprived us of the last opportunity to enjoy the holiday, which we had eagerly awaited for so long. Feeling oppressed, we unanimously burst out cursing the governess. Misha rushed to her bed, the rest of us close behind him, and the bed was shortly turned upside down. We dragged the feather mattress to the floor, beat it, stamped on it, and spat on it with such frenzy, as if the oppressor herself were before us. Having satisfied our first angry impulse, we calmly began to discuss our plans for revenge. We scattered trash and poured water on her bed. We let cockroaches and other insects loose on it. We used her pillows to wipe the entire floor. Finally, after covering everything with a blanket, we settled down. But Misha said it was not enough. He came up with the idea of luring her into the nursery in the dark and tripping her. We accepted his proposal with delight. Misha was a master in the art of tripping: he mowed down his victims like ears of wheat! We put out the night-light and poured the lamp oil on the path that the governess had to walk to her bed. Misha hid by the door. To attract our prey, we joined hands, formed a circle, and started jumping and spinning like mad, shouting, whistling, and screeching frantically. Our hair was flying—nearly undressed, we looked like dancing savages preparing for a sacrifice. Recognizing the sound of her charges, the governess escaped the arms of her beau and rushed to the nursery. We were already lying quietly in our beds when, after opening the door and stepping over the threshold, the governess was suddenly sprawled out on the floor with a squeal. We could hardly breathe—some of us called out, as if half asleep. When someone brought light, the governess rushed to the candle and wildly examined her dress, which, to her horror, was covered in oil. She nearly cried. This misfortune came as such a surprise that she lost her usual shrewdness. She tried various fixes, but soon sadly realized that there was no way to save the dress, and it was impossible to appear before company in it. She undressed in despair and, to comfort herself somehow, ordered us to kneel by her bed. Pleased with our good luck, we surrounded her happily. She tossed and turned in bed. The music choked her; she would have given half her life to return to the hall, but there was no other dress. She closed her eyes and tried to fall asleep. We squeaked plaintively (*"Mademoiselle, pardonnez-moi"*), and for the first time our cries, which had given her obvious pleasure in the past, tormented her. She angrily forbade us from asking forgiveness. But we deliberately amplified our squeaking. We all squeaked, though Misha said *"Pardonnez-moi"* in a strangely hoarse voice. Finally, she lost patience and let us go back to bed, promising to deal with us tomorrow. We lay down, but for a long time stayed up whispering, sharing the details of our triumph. The governess didn't sleep, either. For a long time, she coughed and tossed around—whether due to the strong sensations left by the dance or the consequences of her unfortunate fall, I do not know. Or perhaps the creatures we had unleashed on her mattress also contributed to her insomnia. For the first time in our lives, we fell asleep with a vague sense of pride and might.

Chapter Four

THE NEXT DAY, the governess learned the whole story and left us all without dinner. She tried to punish Misha more severely, but his vengeful threats suggested the impossibility of fighting such an enemy. The governess announced to Mama that she could no longer manage the older boys, and Misha was sent to the gymnasium. Once he put on his uniform, he became even more arrogant. Even my younger brothers and I were frightened of him: he mercilessly twisted our arms, pinched us, and hit us with a rope. He was rude to our aunts and the governess at every turn. His studies did not progress very well, but he could make little boxes, invent riddles, and play Three Card Monte, which he taught us all. He was also fond of and skilled at memorizing poems.

Misha went to the gymnasium reluctantly, always accompanied by dogs, which he lured with bones that he kept in his pockets. He would walk right in the middle of the street, looking back with pleasure at the pack running after him. After finding the right spot, he would throw the bones to start a fight. The hungry dogs greedily rushed at the bones, tearing them away from each other, wheezing, baring their teeth, and sparring. My brother lost himself in the spectacle, watching with interest from his perch on a curbstone. When the dogs' rage subsided, he would provoke them again. So it happened that, in his investigations of the characters of dogs, he often skipped class, and the winning dog, the most daring and venturesome, was awarded a piece of beef as a badge of distinction.

Around this time, a very ugly, insignificant, and poor suitor began courting Aunt Elena Petrovna; he was counting on the bride's dowry and our father's patronage. He proposed through a matchmaker and never showed his face. But Aunt Elena Petrovna would have married a monkey. Mama was delighted to pawn her sister off on a man who could not offend her own self-esteem with his virtues. And so the business was settled before the matchmaker could open her mouth. There was a terrible fuss preparing to receive the bridegroom. At last, he appeared: short, red as a boiled crab, with a smile pasted on his face, so that one corner of his mouth was perpetually stuck under his ear. His gaze was dull and unctuous. Mama introduced the bridegroom to Elena Petrovna, who was seeing him for the very first time, and from that day on she was betrothed. Our governess was completely overtaken by envy: she became inattentive in lessons, her mind elsewhere. We talked back to our aunts with impunity. Once, they quarreled with the governess over me. The bride had ordered me to lace up her dress and I refused. She left me without tea. I got angry and said that we couldn't wait for God to deliver us from at least one aunt, and I promised that when she was gone, I would light a candle to Nicholas the Wonderworker. The sensitive bride teared up. Her sister would not stand for this: like a hawk extending its talons, Stepanida Petrovna moved to grab my hair, but I managed to save myself by quickly throwing my apron over my head. Pale with anger, she pounded on my head until I saw stars, but I laughed and assured her that it didn't hurt at all. Then she, too, burst into tears and demanded that the governess severely punish me. To my surprise, the governess gave me a very delicate reprimand—that was all. The bride and her sister were indignant at this light punishment and attributed such indulgence to envy. Turning beet red, the governess contemptuously announced that such trash was not worthy envying, and if she wanted to, she could find a better and more clever bridegroom. Such a contemptuous review of my aunt's betrothed filled the sisters with a terrible rage. A violent quarrel broke out that could have easily ended in bloodshed, but, fortunately, Aunt Alexandra Semyonovna arrived in time and separated them. The next day, Mama received two complaints: both sides claimed they had been insulted.

The bridegroom visited us every evening. Upon arriving, he would kiss his bride's hand, sit down in the corner, respond mindlessly to questions—never working up the courage to pose any in return—drink two cups of tea with rum, rise, kiss the bride's hand again, and go home. One evening he was redder than usual, smiling more broadly, and he eyed his bride in a strange way. To everyone's surprise, he even asked two questions: one was whether it was possible to give him rum without tea. After settling in the corner, he walked with uneven steps toward his bride, who, thinking that he was going to take his leave, extended her hand to him as usual. But instead of kissing her hand, he kissed her on the lips. The bride recoiled and the bridegroom, having lost his balance, stumbled over the governess standing nearby. She jumped back with a squeal, and the bridegroom fell to the ground, sprawling. We came running at the governess's screeches. Standing in the corner and covering her face with her hands, she shouted, "Oh, *ma chère*, he tried to kiss me!"

The bridegroom stood up, smiled, bowed, and left the room. My enraged aunts attacked the governess for daring to accuse the bridegroom of such a shameful intention. Stepanida Petrovna screamed especially loudly, but the governess looked at her with such insulting amazement that my aunt bit her tongue and glared at her sister. The governess told the bride, "*Ma chère*, kindly tell your betrothed not to forget himself and to behave more decently around a well-born woman!"

Pale with rage, Elena Petrovna responded, "What makes you think, *ma chère*, that he wanted to kiss you? He stumbled—it was an accident!"

"Quite right, an accident! You probably didn't notice how he stretched his lips out to me, but, thank God, I managed to push him away. The poor thing, so weak today that he fell over . . ." The governess began to laugh.

"That's not true, you're lying," the bride objected passionately.

"I'm sorry you don't believe me, but I've been meaning to tell you for a long time that he looks at me too intently, as if I'm the one he's marrying. I confess that I am not used to such things, and I'm very embarrassed . . ."

The bride sobbed with jealousy. Aunt Alexandra Semyon-ovna tried to stop the quarrel, but Elena Petrovna's tears won out over Stepanida Petrovna's jealous anger. She could no longer stand it and picked a fight with the governess. "Tell me, please, how long have you been so very embarrassed? I've seen how you throw yourself at everyone!"

"What! Throw myself? No, I'm sorry, *ma chère*! I'm not like you; I won't allow Pyotr Lukich to kiss me. I saw you two bidding each other goodnight in the front hall yesterday . . ."

Stepanida Petrovna jumped up, came up very close to the governess, and shouted menacingly, "Who do you think I am? Go on, say it! See, she thinks she's so important, just because she knows French!"

"This is too much, *ma chère*, you're forgetting yourself! Only chambermaids speak that way!"

"So I'm a chambermaid! You dare to call me a chambermaid?"

After that I couldn't even understand what they were saying, all the ways they were berating each other. Finally, hearing the screams, Mama sent a man to tell them to quiet the children. They resumed their quarrel in whispers, supplementing their words with looks and gestures.

After she learned what the bridegroom had done, Mama hurried to finish the matter and gave her sister money for a dowry. In this the bride demonstrated such expertise and foresight that one might assume she was getting married for the third and final time. No custom was forgotten, no trifle missed. She bought cloth from which bed sheets were cut, so long and wide that each could have served as a sail for a large ship. Shirts were cut and sewn to fit the bridegroom, who, by order of the bride, brought his shirt one evening for measuring. After he left, the governess sarcastically asked her, "*Ma chère*, were you not ashamed to handle a man's shirt?"

"Why not? He's my betrothed!" she answered with pride. Every evening Elena Petrovna and her sister sewed shirts for the bridegroom. Whenever anyone passed, she drew their attention to this work.

It came time for furnishings. The bride went with her sister to a new apartment that the bridegroom had prepared. I asked to go with them, and they gladly took me along because they needed someone to carry things. We entered a set of small, low-ceilinged, half-empty rooms. The smell of varnish and wood announced the presence of new furniture. At the sight of the double bed, the bride exclaimed, "Oh, just look at it! Short and narrow! One of us is bound to fall out! Even in the shop I said it was small, but you said to the merchant, 'Fine!'"

Stepanida Petrovna, irritated by her younger sister's wedding preparations, took offense and, bursting into tears, said, "So that's how you thank your sister for all her troubles!"

The bridegroom came in, red-faced as usual, and consoled her with a smile.

"Come now, don't cry, Stepanida Petrovna. . . . By God, it will be fine!"

Drying her tears, she threw herself on the bed, stretched out to her full height and asked the bride, "What do you think? Is it too small? Still think there's not enough room? Hm?"

Reassured, Elena Petrovna went to look at her other purchases, jealously inviting her sister to follow her. But when she unfolded the blankets, she turned pale again and threw up her hands.

"Oh, he's shameless! He palmed off two small blankets instead of the single comforter!"

And then, throwing one blanket aside, then the other, the bride began to cry and complain about her misfortune and all the people who, without exception, wished her ill. The ruddy bridegroom smiled again and said, "Come now, don't cry, Elena Petrovna! By God, it will be fine!"

I listened to their conversation very attentively, walked around the bed, and determined that it could easily fit all the wedding guests. When I returned home, the laundress and the maid asked me about the bridegroom's apartment. I told them everything in detail.

On the eve of the wedding, the bride, the laundress, and the maid to the bathhouse and invited the governess. When they returned four hours later, the bride was finally a perfect match for her bridegroom: just as red in the face. That evening, Stepanida Petrovna lost her head and started whispering and winking at the governess. The bride grew angry and occasionally said, "Why, I never! Forgive me, you're mistaken!" The next morning, she received a visit from her mother, our grandmother, who kept whispering to her. Elena Petrovna rudely answered, "I know everything!" But Grandma kept whispering. Evening came. The bride began to dress. Our aunt and the governess vied to hand her pins for her hair and gown. Finally, fully dressed in her wedding gown, Elena Petrovna was led to the hall, filled with guests in their finery. Her mother and father began to bless her, and, to my surprise, she suddenly began weeping. They took her to the church in tears, leaving us behind, even though we cried as much as she did.

An hour later the whole house was bustling. The bride solemnly entered the hall on the arm of the bridegroom, who looked like a crab in a white tie. They were seated at a luxuriously decorated table and champagne was served. The guests shouted something, and the couple kissed. I felt so ashamed that I ran to the entresol and went to bed. A wild roar woke me up; I ran downstairs with sleepy eyes and saw the bride and bridegroom kissing again. The red-faced guests, glasses in hand, drowned out the frantic music with their clamor. Everyone stood up from the table and began bidding the newlyweds farewell. The old folks were gone: they had been driven home in a carriage long before, probably too tired to stand. Mama took their place, kissing the bride on the forehead, making the sign of the cross and wishing Elena Petrovna a good night. Then the guests began saying goodbye, smiling strangely. . . . There would have been no end to these goodbyes and well wishes if the bride herself had not dragged away her bridegroom, who followed her with a dull look and a stagger.

When I awoke the next day, I was shocked to discover that our aunt had not spent the night at home. When the newlyweds paid a visit, Mama greeted them with a gift, quite an expensive one. Talking with her, the bride blushed, and the red-faced bridegroom's perpetual smile was bigger than usual. . . . They entered the nursery. The bride's haughty look irritated the governess, who, after congratulating her, said very loudly, "No doubt you are tired, *ma chère*? You're so pale . . ."

The bride looked at her contemptuously. "Yes, *ma chère*, very tired!" Elena then quietly added, "You're always talking nonsense!"

The wedding came at a cost for me. I often ran outside the front hall to see the lampions burning and likely caught cold; by evening my head felt heavy and my bones ached. I didn't sleep that night, burning with fever, and during the day I lay in a state of near oblivion. At first, they didn't believe me, said I was pretending, that I was lazy, and tried to make me sit in lessons. But when they noticed I wouldn't eat anything, they relented. I had a debilitating fever that made me weaker by the day. Neither of my parents noticed that I'd been missing for two weeks, and no one dared to tell them about my illness because my mother always scolded Aunt Alexandra Semyonovna when she requested money for medicine: "You should have given them more to eat!"

Like a sexless being, neither a girl nor a boy, and unloved by anyone, I was left to nature. One incident proved a turning point in my illness, perhaps even saved me from death. I was lying in a fever next to my brother, who was sleeping sweetly. Everything was quiet. The breathing of my siblings terrified me. It seemed as if they were not sleeping but had died, and they were lying not in beds but in graves. When I closed my eyes, it seemed to me that it wasn't my brother but a giant cockroach lying beside me, touching me with its antennae. I sat up in bed and looked around in a frenzy, surprised at myself. I woke up my brother, who asked, half-asleep, "What's wrong, Natasha?"

"I'm frightened!"

"Then put the blanket over your head!"

With that, my brother fell instantly back asleep. I took his advice and lay there for a long time, trembling from visions. Suddenly I heard a knocking in the hall. The door to the vestibule opened loudly, and an unfamiliar gasping voice shouted, "Water, there's a fire, fire!" My hair stood up on end. Soon there was a bustle, doors slamming, and everyone was running around. I was sure that if our room caught fire, they would forget me. I was too sick to escape alone, and I realized that I had already started to burn. I wanted to scream but couldn't . . .

Suddenly the door creaked, and my father appeared, pale, holding a candle in one hand and blocking the light with the other. He slowly began to walk around the beds and look at the faces of the sleeping children. When he came to me, I sat up and gave him a pleading look. I wanted to ask him to save me, but his stern, cold gaze struck me dumb. He asked, "Why aren't you sleeping?" Trembling all over, I replied, "I'm afraid of fire!" He frowned and said in a frightening voice, "If you dare wake anyone up . . ." Then he pulled the blanket off me and used it to cover the window, which had already begun to shine with a reddish sheen. Then he went around again to examine his children. I watched him closely. Terrified, I waved him over with a pleading motion, but he wagged his finger at me, then left quietly and locked the door behind him. A minute later, I heard the firemen coming upstairs and the crack of the wall collapsing. I held my nose and closed my eyes to block out the smoke that filled the room. I was suffocating. . . . Then the entresol caught fire. I felt it burning me, saw my sleeping brothers and sisters in flames, and in the middle of the room a huge black cockroach was squealing and spinning around. At last, my father appeared, with a terrible smile, and wagged his finger at me. Suddenly the entresol collapsed on me with a thunder and crash . . .

When I awoke, it was the afternoon. My head was bandaged, and Aunt Alexandra Semyonovna was sitting by my bed. A doctor came in, followed by Mama. He looked at me attentively, took my pulse, and, bending down, asked whether I felt hot. I told him I wasn't and asked for some water. Mama herself gave me something to drink, but I was no longer thirsty and told her I was tired. The doctor felt my head and said to Mama, "Almost no fever. Nearly gone. She won't be delirious anymore. Well, thank God, your daughter is saved! What upset her so, and why was her illness so neglected?"

"Really, I don't know. She went to bed healthy, and in the morning, she started screaming that she was burning and that her brothers and sisters were on fire!"

On his way out, the doctor said, "You should look after her now!"

Mama was apparently offended by this advice and, following him out, grumbled, "Honestly, I don't know what more I could do for them!"

Chapter Five

THE CONCERN SHOWN FOR ME ended abruptly. As soon as the doctor said, "Your daughter is saved," I was left to nature, which for its part tried to justify the powers with which it had been so flatteringly vested. Soon I was sitting in lessons like before, going hungry and kneeling for five hours in a row. Ever since the wedding, the governess had been growing thinner. The evenings became boring; Stepanida Petrovna visited the newlyweds, and Aunt Alexandra Semyonovna wasn't one for friendly outpourings. During lessons the governess seemed lost in thought, sighed, and often took up her pen to write. Finally, one morning, during lessons, she announced to our aunts that she intended to leave us. She read out her new terms, filled with details and considerations that proved her deep knowledge of practical life:

"I, the undersigned well-born maiden, in possession of a certificate, undertake to teach seven children, boys and girls,

French and German, history, geography, arithmetic, the law of God and all other subjects; to teach the girls good manners and music, and the boys decency, politeness, and, if necessary, dance. In return, I am to receive one thousand two hundred a year in banknotes, and a covered spring carriage every other Sunday; I am to be treated as a noble maiden; the relatives of the children, if there are any, should behave as politely as possible around me, and the servants should rise when I pass by and refer to me not according to their whims but as 'Miss.' I shall dine at the same table as my employer, at a seat in the middle, not the end, of the table. Tea and coffee four times a day. A separate room with decent lighting and furniture; a girl at my complete disposal who can comb hair, dress, and sew, and another girl of ten years of age who can knit stockings. Thread for two dozen stockings, linen for a dozen shirts, a dozen double bedsheets."

"*Ma chère*, double bedsheets? Why do you need those?" interrupted Stepanida Petrovna. "Are you really hoping to get married?" She laughed sarcastically.

The governess blushed and declared that double bedsheets were more valuable, so that's why she had asked for them; but as our aunt continued to tease her, she finally exclaimed, "So, what if I do want to get married? What's so strange about that! If your sister got married, why can't I?"

"To whom?" our aunt asked ironically.

"Goodness, *ma chère*! How would I know? Well, perhaps to some landowner or other . . ."

Stepanida Petrovna turned pale. "A fine landlady you'd make!" she whispered. The governess was so caught up with the idea of becoming a landowner's wife that she forgot to finish writing out her conditions. She fell into thought, tilted her red head to one side and, smiling, drew something on a scrap of paper. Later we saw it all covered with "Landlady of such-and-such village," followed by her name and patronymic, and then several dots, probably placeholders for her future spouse's surname, and finally, a magnificent flourish, or simply "Landlady, Landlady."

Our joy was so great that we did not believe our luck until the day of the governess's departure. I felt very sorry for the girl she had demanded to be put at her full disposal, and for the poor children who could not foresee the thirst and hunger that awaited them. The governess's goodbye to Stepanida Petrovna was very touching (they even promised to write to each other as often as possible), but Mama, dissatisfied with the governess for leaving and thus temporarily disturbing the order of the house, parted with her coldly. Taking her leave from us, the governess shed tears; but when she saw our faces beaming with joy, she was so upset by our insensitivity that she would certainly have punished us if they hadn't been hurrying her to leave.

When my father returned home that evening, we heard our mother's voice and the governess's name. We quietly approached the door. Mama was saying heatedly, "Just try to find someone who will look after this trash!"

Anticipating an unpleasant conversation about the children, my father gave a displeased grimace and said lazily, "Well, hire another one!"

"No, sir, I beg your pardon! I've suffered enough with that one! I'm being driven to an early grave by these endless troubles and worries!"

And Mama burst into tears, which always worked wonders at times like these. Our father, immediately frightened, did not dare contradict her.

"Come now, do what you want, then." And, with a dismissive wave, he propped his head on his hands. Mama turned to Kirilo Kirilych and spoke for a long time about how her children tormented her, then concluded, "It's time to send them all to schools. . . . At home they just fool around. Misha skipped school again today. You, Andrei, if only you'd whip him . . ."

"That boy doesn't respond to lashes," said my father, who then lay his head on a pillow, letting everyone know that he was now completely indisposed to talk about childrearing.

"I'll give them all away!" exclaimed Mama fervently. "The girls can leave off with books and take up sewing; I've gotten by without books, God grant them the same; Lord knows who will marry them, never mind that they're educated!" Mama chuckled. "I'll send Mikhail to a teacher, perhaps he'll whip him into shape. . . . What else? Andrei, are you listening?"

My father gave an emphatic grunt. Mama continued, "We'll send Fyodor to my brother Semyon; he can learn how to paint."

Then she stopped, waiting for inspiration to strike.

"And how old is your Natalya?" asked Kirilo Kirilych.

Mama was confused. Always lying about her own age, she had completely lost count of her children's.

"Ten, I think," she answered—incorrectly, since I was already twelve.

"And Ivan?"

Mama became angry.

"God only knows how old they all are!"

My father, thinking by the sudden volume increase that his wife was asking him something, gave another grunt. Kirilo Kirilych suggested sending me to music school.

"Excellent!" exclaimed Mama. "And we'll send the two younger ones to the gymnasium, with full board. All right, Andrei?"

Instead of an answer, we heard a snore.

"Do you see?" Mama exclaimed angrily. "Everything falls to me!"

Having learned of our fate, we ran to Aunt Alexandra Semyonovna, surrounded her, and started talking all at once about where everyone would be sent.

"They're sending Misha to a teacher."

"That's fine! But, Auntie, tell them that if they beat me, I won't study. . . . I'll join the army!"

Misha spoke so decisively that our aunt became frightened and began to persuade him against it.

"And Fedya will be sent to Uncle to learn how to paint."

"Yes, brother, he'll teach you how to paint signboards."

"And Natasha and I will be traveling musicians . . . to help Mama."

"And you, Auntie, she'll send you and Stepanida Petrovna to become dancers. . . . You'll play Sylphide . . ."

"Stop talking nonsense."

Our aunt grew cross. We laughed, and Misha threatened more and more fiercely to leave for the Caucasus.

"Then go, brother!" shouted the future musician. "I'll compose a march for you when you're a regimental commander."

We spent the rest of the evening discussing our future lives. Our younger brothers, Pyotr and Boris, wept bitter tears. The next day, Aunt Alexandra Semyonovna stuttered that we were still very young, to which Mama answered angrily, "Pamper them! 'They're still very young!' At their age, you know, some children are already feeding their parents!"

It's true: at that time, two boys hardly older than my brothers were touring Europe giving concerts and earning a lot of money. They also visited Saint Petersburg. For the first time ever, Mama reserved a box and took us with her. Throughout the entire concert she kept up a constant refrain about how some children feed their father, and there's only two of them while she has eight, who can't do anything except cause her grief.

Our sorting was over almost as soon as it began. Misha was sent to a teacher, whom Mama had chosen according to her own tastes. Dressed in their new uniforms, my younger brothers sobbed as they parted with their toys, which they had given me for safekeeping, charging me with seeing that they were collected from the gymnasium as early as possible on Saturday. Alexandra Semyonovna also shed tears and gave them ten kopecks each. The next day Mama severely reprimanded her for pampering the boys, and Alexandra Semyonovna returned to her room in tears. We openly denounced and cursed the spies, knowing very well that Alexandra Semyonovna had been told on by the gossiping Stepanida Petrovna, who always ran to her mother after such feats and returned only the next day when the storm had subsided.

We did not like the uncle who took in Fyodor, as he was an exceptionally coarse person. He thought that our brothers weren't being whipped enough, and would say, "If they let me have a try at you, then you'd really get it!" His voice trembled with such emotion, one would think that whipping his nephews was his life's most cherished wish. Uncle Semyon's appearance was very striking: his face was long and pockmarked, and he always looked deep in thought. His nose was big and looked crudely made. His arms and legs were all clumsy. His small gray eyes were so empty and expressionless that when he wasn't moving his limbs, he could be mistaken for a poorly made scarecrow. His rude nature and lack of education were evident in his every step. His gait was firm and slow—he always held one hand behind his back, as if it were permanently attached. When he came to the nursery, he kissed his beloved niece Sonya on the forehead and for decency's sake kissed Katya as well. "Well, hello, Sonya. Hello, Katya . . ." When my turn came, he turned his back and said dryly, "Well, hello, *Mamselle* Natalya." Then he inevitably exclaimed, "Oh, my lower back hurts, Sashenka!", his name for Aunt Alexandra Semyonovna. "Oh, Sashenka, my hemorrhoids!" He treated his own sister, Stepanida Petrovna, quite coldly. They did not like each other, and she openly mocked him. Uncle Semyon was very fond of telling stories, despite the fact that no one could understand him when he spoke. Whenever he finished a story, he laughed loudly. I always joined him: I was terribly amused by his thoughtful expression and his confidence that he spoke intelligently. He once happened to be in Kursk for some time, but he gleaned very little information from the experience.

"Imagine that, Sashenka. . . . Ha, ha, ha! You can buy a pound of grapes for ten kopecks, ha, ha, ha! Here, they're rubbish, but in Kursk I saw bunches a yard long . . ."

"Is Kursk a nice city, Uncle?" I asked with a smile.

"It certainly is! They shove grapes in your face everywhere you go, it's true, and each bunch is a yard long. Even peasants eat grapes there. . . . Ha, ha, ha!"

Uncle Semyon lived with his parents. I often visited my grandma and saw how they lived. Their apartment was small, only three rooms and a kitchen, no servants: Grandma herself fulfilled the duties of cook and maid. Grandpa had his favorite activities, which he refused to share with anyone else: stoking the fire and polishing the samovar, candlesticks, and knives. Uncle Semyon was a painter. He had a post in the Senate's heraldry department that didn't occupy much of his time, and he had very little private work. He spent his time laying out grand solitaire, slowly smoking a short pipe, and biting his nails, which were so disfigured that it made me sick to look at his hands. And sometimes, with his hand behind his back, he would walk around the room and hum: "A young sailor, rigger he was . . ."[1] He sang with a sadness that frightened me. I snuggled up to Grandma and asked her to tell me a story. However, it was sleep that played the main role in Semyon's life. He often went to bed after dinner and woke up the next day in the evening, and even then only thanks to Grandma, who, afraid that her son had not eaten in so long, would finally decide to give him a shake. He would open his swollen eyes and say, "Why are you bothering me with your tea? A man can't get a wink of sleep around here! As soon as your head hits the pillow they're saying, 'Get up, Semyon!'"

Only when he came over to our house was he fully convinced that a new day had long since begun.

"*Mamselle* Na-ta-lya, give me today's showbill."

I gave him the showbill. Having thoughtfully contemplated the date written on it, he burst out laughing.

"Ha, ha, ha, Sashenka! I went to bed on the seventh, and now it's the eighth. . . . Ha, ha, ha!"

This is the man to whom Mama entrusted Fyodor's education. Uncle Semyon greeted our brother with these words: "Well now, brother Fyodor, don't be lazy, or I'll flog you." And he kept his word, beating and whipping the poor boy so much that he developed a stutter. When Fyodor came home, he seemed like a village idiot.

"So, Fedya, did you get whipped this week again?"

"Yes . . . fi-ive . . . times," he answered, his voice terribly strained.

I cried when he returned to our uncle.

Fortunately for Fyodor, he was pampered by our grandma, whom we all loved. She brought us a present each Sunday, treated us with kindness, and never lectured us.

When Semyon noticed that Grandma was feeding Fedya on the sly, he scolded the boy and threatened to lock him in a room. At first, he whipped the boy with twigs from the broom, but Grandma grew angry and kept the broom away from her son, insisting that she needed it to sweep the kitchen. Tired of borrowing the broom and noticing the crafty old woman smuggling thin straw brooms from the bathhouse, our uncle bought a whole cartload of twigs from a Finn who was always yelling, "Brooms, get your brooms!" in the courtyard. Our uncle ordered the new switches to be placed in the storeroom with the firewood, and when he saw our mother, he demanded that she reimburse him for them.

CHAPTER FIVE

Angry over some crooked line Fedya had drawn, our uncle ordered him to fetch some switches from the storeroom: "And good ones, too, otherwise I'll fetch them myself, all the worse for you!" Fedya left in silence, as if he'd been ordered to fetch a glass of water. At first he had tried to appeal to his torturer's emotions, crying, falling on his knees before him, begging. But the torturer would walk slowly around the room, smoking silently, not paying any attention to our poor brother. The pale, trembling, blue-lipped boy would continue to moan and sob, begging to at least postpone his punishment, but our uncle kept silent. In despair, our brother would crawl on his knees behind our uncle and kiss his feet—nothing helped! Finally, Fedya gave up his useless attempts. Without being asked twice, he would go to ask Grandma for the key to the storeroom.

"Really, Fedya, again?" she asked in horror.

"Yes, Grandma, ag-gain." And our brother cried, touched by her compassion.

"Well, I'm not giving you the key. . . . Tell that to the villain!"

But Fedya begged her to give him the key: "It will be worse. He'll whip me to death!"

Grandma ran with Fedya to the storeroom, repeating, "My God, my God! This life of mine! The child's being tortured, and I stand here watching, even handing over the switches. . . . This is worse than hard labor!" Taking out a bunch of rods, grandmother and grandson began to select a few.

"Here's a good one, Fedya," she said.

"Are you crazy, Grandma?" he replied, fearfully tossing aside the thin rod to avoid temptation.

"Well, then this one . . ."

"No, Grandma, stop! I'll choose for myself. All the ones you pick are thin and brittle . . ."

And he diligently chose the best birch rods.

Uncle grinned when Fedya returned. Pipe between his teeth, he took the rods and lovingly examined each one, swinging it through the air so that it bent and whispered gently into his ear. He responded to each switch with an affectionate smile, as if it were the woman he loved. Meanwhile, Fedya was arranging a sort of gallows for himself: he took a plank, put it on two chairs, and tied them tightly together; then he lay down on the plank to test its strength. Having prepared himself as required, Fedya alternately flushed and paled as he awaited his torture. Uncle paced slowly and smoked. After finishing his pipe, he said, "Lie down." With a shudder, glancing at the executioner's stern face, Fedya silently complied, clasping the board with his hands and pressing it tightly to his heart, which wanted to jump out of his chest and knocked loudly on the board like a pendulum. Having rolled up his sleeves and stretched his arms and legs, the torturer raised his arm . . .

Uncle finally shouted, "Get up," and went to fill his pipe, singing, "A young sailor, rigger he was . . ." His mournful song was accompanied by Fedya's sobs. Uncle stopped for a minute, asking, "Did the trick, eh?" and then carried on singing.

When Grandma saw her tortured grandson, she burst into tears and bemoaned her cruel fate. She gave Fedya a pie hot from the oven and promised to make him coffee after dinner. Then she approached her son, tried to persuade him to stop, and called him a murderer and a brute. She left in despair.

"You villain, who do you possibly take after?"

"Certainly not you!" Semyon shouted back with pride.

Our grandpa also tried to protect Fedya once, but his son darkly warned him not to interfere with his business. Grandpa, a great coward, would run into the front hallway, covering his ears, and shout, "Oh my God! He'll kill him! He'll kill him! Who taught the scoundrel to hit like that? I never laid a finger on him . . ." The first such scene caused a commotion throughout the building; hearing the frantic screams, the neighbors leaned out of their windows with alarmed faces. But they soon grew accustomed to such scenes, and finally my brother, seeing that his screams only made Uncle more bitter, stopped making noise. After that, the punishments occurred in silence. Only the boys living with the tailor continued to follow our uncle's feats—which had a beneficial effect on them—with greedy curiosity. Their pale faces brightened noticeably; they not only reconciled themselves to their fate but even thanked God for it, having seen with their own eyes that they could be whipped even more painfully than they already were by their master. For his part, however, the German tailor lost all self-respect, which he'd ceded to our strict uncle. Whenever they met in the hall, the tailor bowed low to Semyon, and when he saw Grandma, said, "Your son is quite a fellow!"

Chapter Six

I LOVED VISITING my grandmother, and the days I spent with her were the happiest of my childhood. I cooked with her, built the fire for supper, and showered her with questions, which my kind-hearted grandma answered with pleasure and affection. In those moments I was completely happy. Grandpa, who constantly grumbled at Grandma, sometimes found fault with me when I dropped or rearranged things, but his anger was limited to grumbling.

Grandpa was about sixty years old, tall and terribly thin. His cheeks were sunken, his legs like dry stalks. He had a long, long nose, crooked as if bent over from thinness. He had small eyes, a huge mouth, and a small head covered with thin brown hair, almost no gray. Such was his appearance. He shaved his beard only once a week—out of economy, but this made him look even more frightening at first glance. His gait was quick and wide. In short, he looked very much like Don Quixote without the calm and majestic facial expression—Grandpa was as cowardly as a child. For ten years he had worn the same sheepskin coat covered with green nankeen, which had grown black and shiny and retained only shreds of fur; and flesh-colored nankeen trousers tied with ribbons at the bottom, thick stockings, and clumsy shoes like galoshes—this was his uniform. But especially striking was his gigantic tie, which made his neck look bigger than his waist. Grandpa had made it himself in a fit of the shakes, when he seemed to think that some demons wanted to destroy him.[1] The tie was unusually thick and elastic, which was intended to delay the action of a hostile rope if it were thrown around his neck. Since then, he never took off his life-saving tie, and if he went somewhere, he tied a kerchief to it. However, such cases were very rare. He did not leave the house more than twice a year, afraid to leave his bed, where he kept all his treasures. After retiring due to illness, he had begun to save his pension in old banknotes under the mattress. Fearing that his money would be stolen and his rum drunk, he didn't allow anyone to touch his bed, which was by the stove. Grandpa would stoke the fire until it was ablaze. Then he would stretch his head toward the stove, grunting with pleasure and grinding his teeth. He didn't notice the fumes, didn't believe they existed. Whenever Grandma lay there unconscious, he attributed her headache to wine, grumbled, scolded her, and quietly sipped rum from the bottle hidden in his bed.[2] Once he started saving money, he began to squeeze Grandma. He'd take out a blue banknote, put it on the table next to him, and tease Grandma with it, saying that her eyes jumped at the sight of money. After muttering for four hours, he'd finally hand over the money but would reproach her for ruining him for the rest of the day.

Grandpa was a reader, though he only read one book: Bruce's Calendar.[3] Holding a magnifying glass to one eye and squinting with the other, he held the book angled away from himself and read aloud that "such and such a Virgo, born between the fifteenth of one month and the fifteenth of another is stubborn, spendthrift, loves fish, prone to luxury; devout on the outside, love-sick on the inside. Once married, she won't love her husband, but will give in to her old inclinations" and exclaimed, "The very portrait of your grandmother!" I asked him to read the entry for his birthday; in his vehemence he began, "A child born between October fifteenth and November thirteenth is by nature cold and wet, with a feminine nature, and is stingy and cruel when angry. . . . Well, Natasha, these things aren't always exact." And Grandpa would close the calendar or redirect the conversation to Grandma, explaining how the words "love-sick on the inside" referred to her passion for wine.

Grandpa tried with all his might to prevent Grandma from going to bed after dinner. Seeing that she would soon be finished cleaning up in the kitchen, he would throw himself on the big bed with chintz curtains that used to be their marriage bed and wait impatiently for Grandma to appear. Whenever I saw him stretched out on the bed, I ran to tell Grandma the bad news. I wanted to lie down and listen to her tell fairy tales and stories from her life. . . . What to do? How to get rid of Grandpa? I would go into his room, drop something loudly and hide behind the door. When he heard the sound, he would jump up and run to his room, and I'd run to tell Grandma that the bed was free. Now it was our turn to lie down and wait triumphantly for Grandpa. He returned, sat down at the table, drummed his fingers, and recited what he had memorized from Bruce's Calendar about how Grandma was a spendthrift, quarrelsome, and prone to luxury. We pretended to be asleep—I pretended to snore—and Grandpa, grinding his teeth, went to his room with a grunt. We laughed softly at our cunning, and I begged Grandma to tell me a story.

Grandma was over fifty years old. Her face still retained signs of her former beauty, despite her long life of hard work, destitution, and wine, which she had taken up in her grief. Grandma's children treated her and Grandpa with contempt. Sometimes, driven to the limit of her patience by their rudeness and her husband's grumbling, she drank an extra glass and threatened to give everyone a thrashing, but even in those moments she was kind to her grandchildren.

"I know, I know everything, Natasha—your mother and father don't love you. All my children are evil, and I'm just a poor . . ." And then she started crying, her tears turning into threats: "I'll kill them all! Natasha, I'm swearing like a drunkard, but even though I'm a drunkard I don't torture my own children. How could I have nursed these snakes in my bosom!" Her voice changed and she continued, "'We're ashamed of you,' they say, 'We don't want to know you!' Yes, well, I don't want to know *you*! Oh, you shameless children! I used to see nothing but black bread at the table for a week, shivered in a cold room with six little ones, with God knows what to drink, nothing to even warm yourself up. Sometimes, Natasha, a neighbor would hear me crying with my nursing baby through the wall, and she'd come by with a glass and beg me to drink: 'You'll have more milk this way,' she'd say, 'and the baby will stop crying.' So, I'd drink it. And it really does warm you up! I slept like a baby. Then your grandfather would come home all stiff from the cold; he didn't have the fur coats your mother and father have. He only had a wool coat—well, you know the one, Natasha."

"Yes, Grandma, the one with the collars?"

"Yes, right! He'd come home nearly frozen. He'd play in the orchestra all day and all evening, and then at night he'd run off to play at some ball or other. Believe it or not, he'd walk home at five o'clock in the morning, didn't have money for a cab. All the man wanted was to warm up and relax, but the room was cold. So, I'd build him a fire and light a candle stump—I'd saved it for him special, spent the entire evening without a fire myself.

"So, there he is, so cold he can't move, just clapping his hands, can hardly warm up. You bring him something from the oven, warm cabbage soup or porridge, whatever's left over from the children. He undresses and starts eating, and what a sorry sight: rail thin, absolutely rail thin. . . . He asks me, 'Nastya, have you eaten?' 'Yes,' I say, while thinking to myself, 'Have you lost your mind? If I'd eaten, there'd be nothing left for you . . .'

"Your grandfather, Natasha, wasn't always as mean as he is now. He'd say, 'Come now, Nastya, I can go to bed without supper, I have something to warm up with.' And he'd pull a bottle out of his overcoat, take a swig, and hand it to me: 'Have a sip, Nastya, you'll warm right up.' At first, my mouth would burn from just one sip, but later I could drink two glasses. Thank God, I kept all the children alive—much good it's done me.

"And when we gave your mother away, we worked day and night so she'd have things better than I did, and now she drives me away. As soon as I step through the door, she says, 'Go to the nursery, Mother, they'll make you punch there.' The way she shames me in front of everyone. . . . And here's another villain, your uncle, the smallpox case. He wasn't always so pockmarked. He was a nice boy—it's as though smallpox spoiled his soul. Well, imagine the grief your grandma suffered! Your grandfather spent God knows how much to save the boy, gave the medic everything we had. And look at the knacker we nursed back to health. If I'd known he'd end up like this, I would have strangled him with my own hands, God forgive me!"

Grandma went to the cabinet, poured herself a glass, downed it in one gulp, winced, and continued, "Oh, Natasha, your grandma had it bad. Sometimes after putting the children to bed, I'd just sit there, couldn't sleep for heartache: Is my son sick? After all, we only had one boy, the rest were girls. I'd stick a nail behind the door, since there wasn't a lock; some shoemaker lived there before us—his boys must have torn off the lock and sold it. I asked the landlord for a new one many times, but he always said, 'What do you have worth stealing?' And he was right: we lived poorly! Your grandfather made a small salary. We just tried to dress neatly and avoid starving to death—not like your mother and father! We had the children's underwear, some old dresses, a warm *capote*—I wore that, all the good it did me in winter! Those were all the riches we could boast of. And even so, we almost came to grief . . .

"One evening when I was alone at home, I heard some rustling. Our building was nasty: all sorts lived there! Tatars, Jews, even runaways would stay there for a few days. You see, they had planned a huge building, but when they were halfway through construction they stopped—Lord knows why, maybe they ran out of money, or there was some lawsuit—and so half of the building didn't have any windows. A whole gang of robbers could hide in it. Different artisans lived there and walked freely through the courtyard. That yard was like a public thorough-fare, thieves galore![4]

"We had a wooden staircase—they weren't going to build a stone one, you know—and it rotted and fell apart. The other tenants and I used a leather ladder for six months. Then we managed to build a staircase out of some old boards—no better than a ladder, really. We'd complain to the landlord, 'We can't even get around in here!' But he'd always say, 'My good people! When you or your children get hungry, you'll find a way to go upstairs!' A dirty thief, that man! Once he took it into his head to put his arms around me, but I taught him a lesson.

"One evening I'm coming back from the shop, a jug of kvass in one hand and molasses for the children in the other. I'm just about to climb the ladder when, lo and behold, I see a red face.

'Where are you coming from?'

'The shop,' I say.

'You're torturing yourself in vain,' he says, 'You're so beautiful; and your husband won't find out, and I'll give you the shoemaker's apartment for the same price, and I'll build a staircase . . .'

"And then he climbs up to me. I tell him, 'Leave me alone, I don't want anything from you,' and he grabs me and gives me a peck on the cheek. I was so disgusted, I could've killed him on the spot. I tell him, 'Oh, you old sinner, I may be poor, but I don't want anything to do with that mug of yours!' And then I threw kvass on his face and scrambled up the ladder. He sneezed, coughed, and started to follow me. But I was young and quicker than him. I managed to get to the door. He climbed halfway up the ladder and then got frightened, but he still swore at me for all he was worth: 'You so-and-so,' he said, 'just you wait! I'll teach you a lesson, sweetheart, for pouring kvass on me. I'll take away the ladder. We'll see how you change your tune when your cubs get hungry.'

"I was scared to death. The children asked for a drink, but only the dregs of the kvass were left, and I was afraid to go back to the store. I thought, 'If he takes the ladder while I'm away, I'll be stuck downstairs.' I struggled to calm the children, hurried to make them tea with molasses, and finally they quieted down."

"Why didn't you complain to Grandpa?" I asked, indignant at the landlord.

Grandma smiled and said, "Your grandfather's a fine one, but he's always been a coward. I once saw him with a thief, and he acted like a little boy. But your grandmother has always been a Cossack, a Cossack, I tell you! Even the thief called me a dashing woman!"

"Grandma! You met a thief, and he didn't kill you?"

"No, he didn't do anything, just gave me a fright. You see, I've seen my share of suffering!"

Grandma propped her head on her hand and fell into thought. After about three minutes, she waved her hand, returned to the cabinet, and drank straight from the decanter. I was surprised she wanted to drink such bitter stuff. Once, out of curiosity, I had tried one drop from an emptied glass, and my mouth burned for half an hour afterward.

"Grandma, Grandma!" I shouted, tired of staring at her back.

Grandma shuddered, quickly put the decanter back in its place, and rattled around some forks and knives, as though she was tidying the cabinet.

"Grandma, tell me about the thief."

"Hold on, Natasha, let me tidy up a bit," she said in a displeased voice. She slammed the closet shut and lay down on the bed, where I had been awaiting her for a long time.

"Oh, oh, oh, Natasha, how tired your grandma is! Today I ran around Haymarket Square. My arms and legs got so stiff, I could hardly carry my bag home."

"Grandma, darling, tell me about the thief!" And I gave her a big kiss.

"That's enough, Natasha, it hurts when you kiss that hard. Listen, I'll tell you the story. Well, where was I?"

"You were sitting alone one evening, Grandma, and heard some rustling," I said, holding my breath.

"Yes, there I am sitting alone, and I hear someone shaking the door. 'Who's there?' I say, thinking it's a neighbor come for a light. No answer! I can tell something's wrong—the door is shaking harder by the second. I think, well, what if it's a thief! He'll steal the last pair of underwear and, for all I know, wake the children. They'll scream, and he'll probably strangle them! A chill ran over me: What do I do? I think to myself, why don't I scream as if someone else is home, so I go, 'Ivan! Ivan, get up! Someone's at the door. Well, then, you, Fyodor, get up and open it!' The thief sneaks away from the door, but a minute later the door starts shaking again. So I shout, 'Come now, get up, look, there's a troublemaker at the door!' I grab your grandfather's old boots, pull them onto my feet, yawn, and stretch. As I walk to the door, my eyes fill with tears and my heart starts pounding. I hear someone going down the stairs, so I swing open the door and scream in a low voice: 'Who's playing pranks here? I'll kill you!'

"After I slammed the door shut, I could barely stand. I put the nail back behind the bottom of the door and put another nail at the top. I started walking around the room, tapping my boots, talking in different voices, sneezing and coughing."

"Was he gone, Grandma?" I was trembling all over.

"Gone? Ha! Listen. It was late evening, I heard more knocking at the door, as if the house was on fire. 'Who's there?' I say. 'Open quickly!' he says, and I was relieved to hear your grandfather's voice. I took the nails out of the door. He was pale and trembling. 'What's wrong, Pyotr Akimych? What's the matter with you?' He struggled to tell me that someone was sleeping in the hall—he stumbled and almost fell. I felt bolder with him around. 'Shine a light, Pyotr Akimych, I'll go see,' and I thought to myself, 'Ah, the thief has gone to sleep!'

"I went out into the hall and saw a huge man in a red shirt, red-haired, snoring on the floor, really making himself at home. I kicked him in his side. He jumped up like a madman, looked around, saw us, and tried to think of how to sneak down. I even felt like laughing.

"I said to your grandfather, who had set the lamp on the floor and then hidden in his room: 'Why didn't you light the way? It's his first time here; he could've fallen!' We laughed. I started making supper and told him, 'Now I'm scared to go into the hall for food—fetch a lamp and let's go together.'

"I pull on the storeroom door but, devil knows, it won't open! So, I bend down and, what do you know, I see a boot sticking out from between the storeroom and the firewood. I hear snoring, so I pull on the boot. Against the firewood, the figure seemed rough and shaggy at first. . . . My word, a house demon? As I say a prayer, a dark, pock-marked, hefty man crawls out. His hair looks like a hat, and his beard is a mess.

'Why are you yelling, woman?' he says. Then he sees your grandfather, who had already run to the doors.

'What are you doing here?' I ask.

'Can't you see I was sleeping?'

'I see that, but do you think this is the place for you? Hm? Go home, if you even have a home, or else!'

"And the thief looks at us closely and then screams, 'What do you mean, or else? What have I done? Did I steal anything from you? Huh?'

"I was frightened. I backed away, and then I screamed at him, 'Quiet, brother, quiet! There's nothing to steal from us!'

'Yes, I see there's nothing here!' the murderer said, scratching his head. He looked into the storeroom. 'Give me a drink of kvass, Auntie, and I swear I'll leave. Nothing to drink, my throat's dry.'

'No wonder you were snoring loud enough to wake the dead!' I told him.

'I know,' he says, 'I was born that way. And it's gotten me into some trouble. . . . But what can you do? As they say, only the grave can straighten a hunchback . . .'

"I had no choice, so I handed him the jug. He drained it, wiped his beard with his sleeve, smiled, and said, 'Auntie, oh Auntie! Give me something to eat, some beef at the very least . . .' And he went into the storeroom himself.

'Oh, you sinner!' I said. 'Breaking fast on a Wednesday?'⁵

'Come now, Auntie, just give me something. The sin will go to my soul—it won't be the first!'

'All right, here.'

"He stuck the piece of beef and bread in his shirt and said, 'Thank you, Auntie. You should have handed it over straight away, instead of shouting at me! You're a crafty broad, but even so I'd get along with you just fine. And I'd break that icicle over there with my little finger,' he said, pointing to your grandfather, who was shaking like a leaf in the doorway. I must admit, I found it all quite funny . . .

'Now then, Uncle, go with God!' I told this fellow. 'Enough horsing around!'

"He put his hat on at a tilt, whistled, and said, 'Goodbye, thanks for the hospitality.' And I thought to myself, 'The pleasure was all mine . . .' For a long time after, I was afraid to be alone in the evenings, in case the thief returned. Early the next morning, I went out into the hall and, what do you know, there's a knife on the floor, a very nice one. I must admit, I was glad—we didn't have a big knife like that, and I thought it'd come in handy at home. Seems I've been cooking with it for twenty years now, it's all worn down . . ."

"Grandma, you clean the greens with that thief's knife?"

But she didn't respond. She closed her eyes, opened them suddenly, and muttered, "I'll give you . . . drunk!" and mouthed the rest of her words without saying them. After a heavy sigh, she started snoring lightly. Then she burst out, "Natasha, Natasha!"

"What's wrong, Grandma?"

"Oh, you're here?" she asked quietly.

"I'm here."

"Well, go to sleep, and your grandma will go to sleep, too. I've tired myself out today! How is my life any better now? Tell me, Natasha, how is it better? The room is warmer and brighter, but . . . Oh, Lord . . ."

Grandma barely finished those last words and then fell silent. The candle flickered terribly; I was agitated. I looked with fright at the wall clock, which seemed to be alive: the monotonous knocking of the pendulum reminded me of my own beating heart. . . . Well, what if it wasn't a clock but a living person whom some sorceress had turned into a clock? And what if I, too, got turned into a clock, to forever hang on the wall—day and night, swinging dejectedly without respite? Frightened, I tried to fall asleep but couldn't. When I opened my eyes again, it seemed like the clock face was smiling at me, and the pendulum was swinging even faster. I turned away, but then I thought that the clock was moving closer, no longer smiling, but blinking plaintively at me. I jumped out of bed, and the clock weights shuddered and knocked about. I ran, and the clock ran after me, knocking.[6] I opened Grandpa's door and shouted, "Grandpa, are you asleep?"

He jumped out of bed and looked around for a long time.

"Ah! Who's there?"

"Me, Grandpa."

"Oh, Natasha? What are you running for? Is your grandmother asleep?"

"Yes, Grandpa."

"You see, what a fancy lady! Asleep right where she lay down to rest after dinner!"

He went to Grandma's room, and I followed him. My fear vanished. Grandpa held a candle to the clock, which was almost at the same height as his head, though the clock was hanging very high.

"Natasha! It's already seven, time to wake your grandmother and put on the samovar!"

I didn't say anything, just stared at the clock and listened to its knocking. Everything was normal. Completely calm, I took out Bruce's Calendar, and Grandpa sat by the bed, drumming his fingers on the table and grumbling until Grandma woke up.

Chapter Seven

SOON I STOPPED visiting Grandma: my brother Ivan and I were
sent to the music teacher every day. Our teacher was a middle-
aged man who was neither intelligent nor educated but quite
kind to us. Our parents had once done him a favor, what sort
I do not know, and Mama very cleverly hinted to him that
now was a fine opportunity to repay her. He agreed to teach
us for free, and since then neither torrential rain nor a blizzard
could stop us: no matter what was done on earth or in heaven,
we went to our music teacher, surprising passersby with our
outfits. My brother wore an overcoat he had long outgrown.
I was forcibly dressed in my mother's old *capote*, with the skirt
hemmed nearly to the waistline, which almost came down to
my knees. I also wore my mother's galoshes, which kept falling
off my feet despite the huge amount of cotton stuffed in them.
Eventually I managed to make sandals out of them, and only
then were they good for anything. In the depth of winter, they

sent us out in high, white, shaggy boots called *vaski*, which slowed down our gait and made us look from a distance like bear cubs broken loose.

Our teacher was married, and his family affairs quite often distracted him from our lessons, to Ivan's indescribable delight. Our teacher and his wife had married for love: he won her heart with his exemplary recklessness. In weather thirty degrees below zero, he spent the whole day pacing below her window. The girl found his self-sacrifice so captivating that, despite her family's resistance, she became his wife. Since then, as proof of her love, she reminded him every day that she had refused many advantageous matches for a poor musician—and our teacher was happy. He trusted her completely, and it was impossible not to, given the incessant tenderness she showered on him in front of everyone. But he didn't know anything about the tenderness she showed another young man in private. The teacher's apartment had only two rooms. The door in between the bedroom and the room where we had our lessons was always slightly ajar, and in the mirror, I often saw the teacher's wife flirting with her husband in front of this young man, and then flirting with the young man when the teacher, breaking free from her arms, returned to us. This young man was nearly living with them. He was very poor, and the teacher's wife was very charitable: she begged her husband to invite the man to dinner every day. They carried on like this until the teacher's wife began to leave in the mornings, claiming she had a headache and needed air. Once, she was not at home, and the teacher was with us. Suddenly the young man ran in, out of breath, and whispered something in the teacher's ear. The teacher turned pale, grabbed his hat, threw on his fur coat, and, still in his dressing gown and slippers, disappeared with the young man. We were very glad that our lesson had stopped so unexpectedly. A few minutes later, the teacher's wife ran into the bedroom, changed her hat and coat and, on her way out, told us, "Don't you dare tell anyone I was here!" The teacher then returned in a frightening rage: he paced the room, clutching his head and repeating, "I'll kill him, I'll kill him, and you, too!" The young man followed him and tried to calm him down, but when he heard that the irate teacher wanted to kill him, he asked in an offended tone, "Why me? How am I to blame?"

"Because you didn't tell me sooner! You said yourself that today wasn't the first time . . ."

Their conversation was interrupted by the arrival of the teacher's wife, who came in smiling and went up to her husband with puckered lips, saying, "Hello, Kokoshka . . ."

Our teacher recoiled angrily and asked in a thunderous voice, "Where have you been?"

"I was taking a walk, Kokoshenka."

"I know you were taking a walk. . . . Not alone, either."

She looked at him with surprise, then at the young man, and said, "You're out of your mind, Kokoshka!"

"No, I'm not!" the teacher exclaimed. "We saw you rush into that sleigh when you saw us. I recognized your black hat. . . . If I'd gotten a cab, I'd have caught up with you, Madam!"

And he walked menacingly around the room.

"When? How? With *whom*? What?" asked the offended wife, raining down questions. "Look what I'm wearing; do you see a black hat anywhere? Look!" And she thrust her yellow hat in her husband's face. The teacher and the young man were confused. The husband ran to look at her coat, and in the meantime his wife threatened to slap the young man, calling him a scoundrel. The teacher brought his wife's coat over and pushed it into the astonished young man's face: "Is this what you call a fur coat?"

The teacher's wife burst into tears and said, "So this is what happens when you pity people and try to do good by them! Listen to me, Kokosha! He has been trying to seduce me for a long time! He wanted to slander me for refusing to deceive you, for threatening to tell you everything."

A cry of outraged virtue filled the room. The young man was apparently stunned by this turn of affairs; he opened his mouth, but his excuses were drowned out by the teacher's screams, threats, and curses: "Out, you bastard! Is this how you repay our hospitality? Get out of my sight, or I'll kill you!"

And it seemed to me that the teacher really was ready to kill the young man, who kept saying, "Please, let me . . ."

"Out! Get out!"

"She's lying . . ."

"Shut up, you scoundrel!"

Meanwhile, the teacher's wife made faces at the young man while standing behind her husband, teasing him in all sorts of ways. Finally, the teacher shoved him out the door, slamming it so hard that it almost shattered. The teacher's wife didn't need much time to change her expression from triumphant to grief-stricken. After recovering from his tense and stormy mood, our teacher was suddenly dumbfounded and did not know how to approach his wife. Finally, after a long silence, he said, "Pipisha, don't be angry that I threw him out."

"What, you think I wanted you to kiss him?"

And she turned her back to her husband.

"Well, forgive me," he said. "I'm a fool, and I'll never be so gullible again!"

"Tell me, how could you have mistaken someone else for me?" Then she smiled.

"You see, Pipisha," he said, "I was so angry, so overcome, I was beside myself. I saw a lady in a fur coat walking with some man. I went up to them, and at that very moment they got into a cab and, as if on purpose, drove off fast. Well, I thought that you . . ."

The teacher's wife burst out laughing. The teacher, seeing his wife, followed suit. And they laughed for five whole minutes.

"Ah, Pipisha!" he said. "Look at me, I'm wearing my house shoes. . . . I went out like this . . . Ha, ha, ha!"

They laughed some more, and then we heard gentle kisses. Remembering us, our teacher sent us home.

From that day on, the teacher gave his wife complete freedom. Very often, after winking at some man from the window, she tenderly bid her husband goodbye and left the house. A minute later, I would see her, not at all far from home, hop into a sleigh with the man and leave.

When the teacher went out to give lessons, leaving us alone at his apartment to practice, the door to our room was closed and behind the wall I could hear a man's voice, the teacher's wife laughing, and the sounds of kissing.

■ ■ ■

CHAPTER SEVEN

We moved to a new apartment; the entresol was no more. On weekdays I was terribly bored, impatiently waited for Saturday, when my brothers would come back home. Sonya and Katya were growing up into young ladies. Aunt Stepanida Petrovna, on the contrary, grew younger, reducing her age by a few years by fixing her hair like my sisters did. She didn't want to seem older than them.

The nursery's monotony was broken only by the visits of a poor official, Yakov Mikhailovich, who usually came to see us when the other guests sat down to cards. He seemed to really like Sofia, who flirted with him out of boredom. But Stepanida Petrovna thought herself the object of his frequent visits, and the hope of marriage flared up again in her heart.

Meanwhile, our uncle visited us more and more often. His passion for cards produced a change in him: he became absent-minded, punished his nephew more rarely, even started dreaming about cards, which had never happened to him before. He did not stand on ceremony with his nieces; after greeting us in his usual way, sitting and talking solely for his own pleasure (because no one else found his words witty or even comprehensible), he would get up, take the candle from the table, and walk away with measured steps. Five minutes later he would return, put the candle on the table with the same calm gravity, rub his hands, and, addressing one of us, say: *"Das ist kalt"*—an expression that represented his entire command of foreign languages. He entered the drawing room, deep in thought.

"Hello, Kirilo Kirilych! Hello, sister!"

"Hello, Semyon," Mama replied coldly.

"Well, then, sister! You won't believe how I whipped Fyodor today." And he kissed his fingers with their chewed-down fingernails. "Good grief! If that doesn't teach him, I don't know what will!"

Semyon would play cards until three in the morning and then pace the room gloomily the next day, muttering to himself, "Oh, I'm a fool, a fool! I should have played the ten!" Or he'd berate the maids.

Once, walking home from lessons, we saw Grandpa on the street. As always, he was wearing his frieze overcoat with its countless collars and a high four-cornered hat with a visor as long as his nose. Grandpa had left the house, and it wasn't even a holiday—we were shocked. We ran up to him.

"Hello, Grandpa!"

He was walking quickly and talking to himself. Our unexpected greeting startled him.

"Eh! Who's that talking to me?" he shouted. Seeing us, he added, "Oh, you two! Well, hello!"

"Are you here to see us, Grandpa?"

"Who else? My own son threw me out. . . . I almost hit him . . . and your grandmother almost roughed him up. . . . Oh, my God! Not for nothing do they say that in terms of spiritual qualities those born under the sign of Saturn are destined to a mean and worthless life. They revel in depravity—that is to say, they possess nothing but worthless qualities, both of body and of soul."

Grandpa was coughing.

"Grandpa, let's go! People are staring."

"Let them stare! I'm not ashamed to say it: my own son drove me out. . . . Bah! How tired I am! I ran here like a madman. What a scoundrel! And your grandmother is happy that her son acts like a madman. No, but what kind of son is he—he's more like an antichrist!" Grandpa shook his head and waved his hands like a madman.

We arrived home. Grandpa insisted on seeing Mama at once. She had been warned about the quarrel between father and son; she greeted Grandpa very coldly and asked, "What is it now?"

"Oh!" Tears prevented Grandpa from continuing.

"Tell me, Father, what's the matter with you and Semyon?"

"Why, I never! My own son just about hit me—that's what things have come to! A scoundrel. . . . He'll whip your son to death!"

"And a good thing, too!" Mama said, looking at us.

"What's a man to do, God help us, when a son drives out his father, a wife curses her husband, a mother rejoices at her son's torture!" Grandpa covered his ears and began walking around the room in a frenzy.

"Tell me, what am I supposed to do?" Mama asked. "You're the one who quarreled with your son!"

"Quarreled?" Grandpa was trembling. "No! He nearly hit me! I'm going to complain!" And he burst into tears.

"Stop talking nonsense!" Mama wanted to leave, but Grandpa held her back, shouting, "Wait! Listen to the father, whose son . . ."

She interrupted him. "What do you want?"

"I can't live with my wife: she's a complete spendthrift! It's hopeless when she's in these moods, she only wants to quarrel . . ."

"Then where do you want to live?"

"Anywhere—just not with her! We've lived together for thirty years, and everything was fine! Suddenly, she's gone round the bend: every day she asks for money, swears at me, 'Why don't you give me enough?', threatens to take all my money. . . . And I don't even have any! Where would I get it? It's the damned wine, I tell you: the woman is a fool, she took to drinking and went mad!"

"I know, I know . . ." Mama interrupted again. "All right, I'll give you a room. Pay me thirty-five rubles a month. You'll have dinner in the nursery. . . . You can stay if you want . . ."

She left without waiting for his answer.

Grandpa thought about it: the thirty-five rubles surprised him, but fear won out over avarice.

"I'd give my last ruble to live apart from those two!" he exclaimed resolutely, only now noticing that Mama had already left. In despair, he added, "So this is what it's come to: my son flies into a rage, my wife curses me, my daughter refuses to listen to me. God Almighty!"

They tried to calm him with vodka. After a drink, he began to speak more clearly: "Today I get up, my wife is hissing like a snake, drunk for the third day in a row! My son comes in, I bow to him and say, 'Quiet your mother, Semyon; she'll be the death of me.' And he holds his pipe in his mouth without a word, the scoundrel, as if he doesn't have a tongue! My wife is screaming and swearing; she comes up to me. I spit and make haste away from that sinner. . . . Of course, she's a fool: if she were drowning in a river, she'd stick two fingers above the water like scissors to show me I'm shaved and shorn . . ."

When talking about female stubbornness, Grandpa always cited the famous fable about the shaved and shorn husband.[1]

"But why did you and Uncle quarrel?" one of us asked.

"Won't let his father warm his old bones!" Grandpa got flustered and started shouting, mimicking his son's voice: "'Don't close the chimney, there will be fumes!'

"I said to him," Grandpa continued, "'So, in your opinion, we're to burn firewood for nothing? To heat the street?' And he screams at me, and my wife, the spendthrift, stands in the doorway, baring her teeth and saying, 'Well done, give it to him, Semyon!' God Almighty, he would've hit me if I hadn't run away from home: better to lose all your things, run from trouble, take to your heels . . ."

"Come now, Grandpa."

"No, for a long time I've noticed that they look at me strangely, eyes full of malice . . ."

Weary of listening to Grandpa, we gradually dispersed and left him alone. Resting his elbow on the table, supporting his head with his hand, Grandpa started grinding his teeth, sipped his punch, and from time to time repeated, "The scoundrel! Drive your own father out. . . . We've lived together for thirty years. . . . Not for nothing do they say . . ." And, for the hundredth time repeating what it was they didn't say for nothing, he finished his glass and lay down.

Due to his sedentary, reclusive life, his illness, and old age, Grandpa was more cowardly and gullible with each passing year. Within a few days, Ivan had gained full control of him: he understood Grandpa so well that he could anticipate his wishes, and only Ivan's answers satisfied our inquisitive grandfather.

Ivan slept in the same room with him. Oh, what plenty Grandpa enjoyed! Donning his white knitted hat, the old man stretched out in bed to his full height, covering himself with a worn wool blanket, so that the only thing sticking out was his thin face and its long, slightly crooked nose. From here he launched into endless stories about how his own son had wanted to throw him out of the house, how he had lived thirty years with a spend-thrift wife, and how on an unlucky day one should not under-take any business. . . . My brother was long asleep, but Grandpa kept talking as long as his tongue could move.

He found a special occupation for himself in the mornings, when the stove was heated. As soon as the fire enveloped the wood, Grandpa armed himself with a long poker, sat down opposite the stove, and watched the growing flame with excite-ment, listening to the crackling of the wood, which echoed his own grinding teeth. The firewood hissed, whistled, and some-times popped. The old man screamed in anger—why was the firewood damp? Why were we wasting so much money? When the pile fell apart, Grandpa lovingly pushed the poker into the flames, tapped the log structure and rejoiced when it caught fire again. Finally, when the wood turned into a mountain of fire, and Grandpa into a rosy charcoal, he raked the coals to one side, looked around suspiciously to see if he was being watched, and, if no one was around, hurriedly closed the chimney and stood by the stove to distract attention from it. How bitterly he regretted that he was not allowed to manage all the stoves in the house!

On Sundays, when our brothers were home, Grandpa could never sit through dinner. For our incessant chatter, which prevented him from speaking, he accused us of willfulness. He praised the olden days when people spoke according to seniority. If we were talking about something interesting, he always wanted to know more details: "Why? What for? How? Who?" He was hard of hearing.

"Eh? What? I can't hear you!" And Grandpa cleaned his ear with his little finger and moved his head next to the storyteller's mouth.

"Well, then, who?"

"Mama lost at cards."

"I hear you, I hear you . . . Why are you shouting as if the house is on fire! So, he came over, and your mother won at cards?"

Vanya quickly relieved us of our tiresome new houseguest. Having read in Bruce's Calendar that between February fifteenth and March fifteenth an attempt on one's life should be feared, Grandpa was very afraid of a violent death. Ivan told Grandpa that on moonlit nights he felt a sort of madness overtake him, and he wanted to strangle and stab everyone. Grandpa looked at the calendar—exactly right! "A boy born under such-and-such planet is subject to fits of madness; beef is very harmful to him."

My brother intentionally held out his plate for seconds, "Auntie, may I please have some more beef?"

Grandpa twisted around in his chair, groaned, and said, "My God! He'll go berserk! He'll go mad! Look: his eyes are already bloodshot!"

My brother shivered, started shaking his head, and stared at Grandpa. The old man jumped up in horror, waved his hands, and shouted, "Possessed! He's possessed!"

That evening, for five hours straight, Grandpa tried to convince our aunt that beef was incredibly harmful, referring to his calendar, but he could not be angry at Ivan for too long; he quickly submitted to his influence and believed only what the boy told him. If my brother wanted gingerbread or biscuits, he went to Grandpa, who was sprawled on his bed and grinding his teeth.

"Grandpa," said my brother.

"What do you want, Vanyusha?"

"My head hurts."

"Then why were you shouting for the whole house to hear? My ears are still ringing!"

"Oh, Grandpa! I can't help shouting; look at the calendar: today's the full moon. . . . Something's come over me, I have a hankering for beef—let's go eat!"

But Grandpa jumped out of bed, rummaged around in it, and pulled out a well-hidden piece of gingerbread.

"Here, take it, but for God's sake, don't eat any beef!"

His grandson ran away satisfied, and the old man cautiously poked his head into the nursery. Convinced that Vanya wasn't there, he surreptitiously told our aunt, "Give Vanyusha some biscuits for tea!"

Auntie tried to reason with him—in vain! Grandpa referred to the calendar, then started on about his scoundrel son, his spendthrift wife, and concluded with the fable about the shaved and shorn husband.

Grandpa was angry that he rarely saw his son-in-law and daughter, but he did not dare complain. Sometimes when our father came to the nursery for breakfast, Grandpa would come out of his room, bow low to him, and say ironically, "Here you are, at last! We haven't seen each other for two weeks. How is your health?"

"Fine, Father. And yours?"

"My health . . . poor!" Grandpa coughed. "This damned cough is suffocating me."

"You should go for a walk—the weather is fine."

"A walk? No, thank you very much."

"Why not, Father?"

"I went for a walk six months ago, and I barely came home alive. All that noise, shouting, commotion! You want to cross the street, they won't let you, the scoundrels! They drive toward you as if they can't see you're walking. And then they shout, 'Out of the way!'—your legs give out from fright! There's a crowd on the sidewalk: 'Hey, can't you see? A bigwig! Make way!'" Grandpa spat to the side and waved his hand. "It used to be that everyone made way for each other, but now they just climb all over you, as if they want to crush you!"

"You've grown old, and you always sit at home; that's why it seems that way to you."

"No, sir, I'm sorry, these are the times we're living in. They say the time will come when brother will be set against brother. . . . Where there is sea, there will be land, whole cities shall disappear, in their place shall grow dense forests, fierce beasts abundant . . ."

"And will that time come soon, Father?" my father asked, laughing.

"You laugh! Everything is funny to you, but Vanyusha. . . . Just the other day he predicted: things will get worse. And he was right! And the northern lights . . ."

"What about the northern lights?"

"I'll tell you: I'm sitting one evening without a candle, and I see the northern lights in the sky, playing. . . . I call Vanyusha over: 'Do you see, Vanyusha?' 'I see them, Grandpa.' 'Well then, is it a good sign or a bad sign?' 'Bad, Grandpa, very bad,' he says. And what do you know? I broke a cup! I don't know how; it jumped out of my hands!"

"I ought to whip your little prophet."

"See, I knew you wouldn't believe me! All you want to do is whip them! As if my own son weren't bad enough . . ."

Grandpa flew into a rage, shouted reproaches and threats, then recalled his scoundrel son and spendthrift wife. Finally, he ran from the nursery in despair, shouting, "Lord, oh Lord, what times!"

Once, to drive Grandpa away, Father brought him some old magazine or other: "Here, Father, read it. It's better than your calendar."

Grandpa accepted the book with a regretful smile. It took him a whole year to read it: whenever he was distracted, he could not find where he left off, and started again from the first page. He marveled at the cleverness of the publisher, who, in his opinion, had composed the huge book alone. He shared his surprise with our servant, Luka, whenever the latter was standing nearby and holding an enormous tray that our aunt filled with glasses of tea. Grandpa apparently considered it humiliating to discuss family secrets in front of a servant and, therefore, their conversations always revolved around literature and politics.

Luka was a very kind man, short, with a smooth bald head and a wrinkled face that resembled an apple that had been frozen and then thawed. Luka had previously served as an orderly in the Turkish campaign, and whenever he told my brothers about his time in the service, he always said, "We took the fortress and we beat the Turks."² Envious of the attention, Grandpa tried to confuse Luka, puzzling him with questions from his calendar and laughing maliciously at his ignorance. But my brothers, to spite Grandpa, would make Luka tell us about his old master and about his campaigns.

"So, we set out on the campaign, here we go, sir. . . . Terrible frost. . . . Some lost a nose, others an ear, a leg. . . . When we reach warm weather, too late to keep 'em! The medic's at your heels ordering: cut it off!"

At the word "cut," Grandpa's face changed, and he quickly interrupted Luka: "The Turks are cunning ones, though they have Easter on a Friday. . . . and the Jews have it on Saturday."

"Yes, sir, I've seen some Jewish girls." And Luka, who was partial to Jewish women, took on a tender expression.³

"So, what, were they good ones?"

"Seems there are none better, though they be unbelievers. . . . Black eyes, long noses, arched brows . . . black, very black. . . . Once the master brought home a Jewish girl: she's crying, chattering in her cursed language, waving her arms. . . . Don't make a lick of sense. She sticks her tongue out at me! She doesn't dare tease the master, so she teases me! Can you believe it! Her father came, fell to his knees. And my master was a fine man. Black eyes, black hair, with the strength of a devil: he could lay you out for three days; you'd be seeing stars. And so," he continued, moving to the table to collect the glasses, "my master started dragging the Jew around, a real joker, 'Well now, you damned Jew, here's your daughter!'"

"Careful, you'll drop the glasses!" Grandpa shouted.

"No, sir, I won't drop them—we carried wounded soldiers on our shoulders during the campaigns, and we didn't drop them!"

"Tea!" called Mama from the other room. She had a surprisingly sonorous voice, which had replaced her bell. Fussing about, the bewildered soldier carried, in place of his wounded comrade, a large tray into the drawing room.

As soon as he left, Grandpa assured my brothers that Luka had been lying, that he didn't know anything. When Luka returned, Grandpa asked him mockingly, "So, you've been to war, but do you know what Saturn is?"

"Of course, sir. We took it by storm."

"You guessed wrong! Saturn is a planet—a planet! Those born under its influence are stingy, cunning, and unsociable!"

"Grandpa, you must have been born under Saturn!"

"Wait, don't interrupt! Unsociable, unloved, unforgiving, but hardworking. . . . In these years, reversals are known to happen: spring is cold, summer is cold and windy, but July is warm. Autumn is cold, but November is warm. The harvests are wet, the spring crops are thin, very little wine, and it's a good time to buy. Thunder and lightning are rare, as are fish. Babies suffer from smallpox, measles, and coughs in the spring, and . . ."

"We know, we know, Grandpa! Let Luka tell us about the Jewish girl!"

But Grandpa continued without pause, trying to shout over the boys: "Great changes in a certain state; a new way of government in a certain republic; a glorious massacre, a great sovereign will reign. And all this is to be expected in 1841 or 1869, or else in 1925."

"Ah, Grandpa! You won't even be alive then. . . . You'll be rotting!"

Grandpa jumped up in horror, clutched his head, and shouted, "You children! You won't let your elder get a word in edgewise!"

My brothers stamped, howled like wolves, and whistled until Grandpa ran to his room, leaving only Luka, who watched his rival's flight with a victorious expression.

"Now, Luka, tell us about the Jewish girl."

"Well, there we are, living. Our Jewish girl cried and cried, then stopped, only she was pale, that's how she was. The master keeps her with him, and his friends tell him, 'Leave her, look at those eyes of hers,' but he says, 'No, I'll break her in!' Once he told her to kiss his hand, and she looked at him like she didn't understand. And I could tell she understood Russian! The master gives you his hand, you kiss it! She shakes her head. And my master, heaven rest his soul, was a hot-blooded man. Once his horse was disobedient. He dismounted, stabbed it in the stomach with his saber, and it fell to the ground! Afterward he himself said that he loved the horse terribly, you know, at the time . . ."

"What about the Jewish girl?"

"Ah!" Luka sighed heavily. "She didn't kiss his hand, fool she was. Would've driven anyone into a rage. The master jumps up and slaps her in the face. She falls to the ground, I'm telling you, like a fly, and then lies there, you know, shuddering. The master leaves, but he doesn't call me after him, so I stay sitting. And what do you guess she does? She falls at my feet. 'Give me a knife,' she says. 'No,' I say, 'I won't.' She's crying all over the place and then brings me money, a lot of it. The master had given her everything; what hadn't he given her? I tell her, 'I'm afraid!' You know, if I give her a knife, she might stab someone. She goes to the bedroom. I hear noises, so I look in and she's hung herself, her legs twitching. I freeze, then run outside and shout, 'Over here, come quick!' Some people came and untied her. She was barely breathing. The master came in, pale as death. He called for a medic, a doctor! They bled our Jewish girl. She opened her eyes and looked around, stunned. . . . After that, she was quiet as a mouse, even cheerful sometimes. She drank wine with the master. Oh, how they used to drink. . . . One night I come home, and the Jewish girl is gone. My master is lying on the floor, covered in blood: his throat had been cut with a razor!"

We had trouble falling asleep that night and had terrible dreams.

Chapter Eight

THE NURSERY'S POPULATION unexpectedly increased. One morning, Mama returned in tears from the funeral of our father's
colleague. Accompanying her was the daughter of the deceased,
a girl of about four. The deceased was a widower: with his death
his daughter had lost her only guardian, and she had no relatives. After much talk of what to do with the orphan, no one
dared to take her. Then Mama stepped forward, drew the little
girl away from her nanny, and, kissing her, said, "Poor orphan,
I'll take your mother's place!"

She pressed the girl to her heart and cried; the child also
started crying and shouted, "Nanny, nanny!"

Although moved, the guests were surprised at my mother's
generosity.

"As if you don't have enough of your own," they said, "you
want to take someone else's!" To which my mother replied with
dignity, "So, in your opinion, we ought to leave the child without

shelter, in the hands of a nurse? No, that's inhumane!" and she wept and kissed the girl, who was busy examining Mama's earrings and toying with her ear.

Mama was very angry that the nurse cried while parting with the child and forbade her from visiting. Our father, noticing the new resident, asked his wife, "Busying yourself with another, then? Don't you have enough of your own?" He paid no further attention to the orphan.

By evening, after playing with dolls, the girl was tired; she called for her nanny, cried, and threw a tantrum. Mama sent her to the nursery and ordered her to be put to bed. The girl was frightened by the many faces she met there and cried out, "I want to go home! Nanny! Nanny!" Her screams were terrible; it was as though she was having a premonition of the fate that awaited her and wanted to escape it. Tired of her ward's cries, Mama herself came to comfort her, but she was inconsolable. Losing her patience, the benefactress threatened to flog the orphan and then left to play cards, informing her guests that the girl was crying for her, and that she was very surprised at the instincts of children, who bind themselves to you forever if you so much as caress them once. . . . The girl, whose name was Liza, completely wore us out. Soon she was running a fever, and no longer cried or screamed, just moaned. Finally, Ivan managed to console her with various stories and assurances that her nanny would come soon. Liza hugged him tightly, laid her burning head on his shoulder, and fell asleep.

From then on, Ivan became her second nanny. She sought his protection whenever one of our younger brothers was chasing her. If she was hungry, Ivan immediately went into a fit of madness, and Grandpa's biscuits satisfied her hunger. She inherited his toys, and he also gave her gifts. When she wanted to see something, and the other children obstructed her view, Ivan lifted her up.

Grandpa also fell in love with Liza. She willingly listened to him and answered his endless questions: What's going on in the nursery, in the kitchen? How many candles are lit, are the stoves closed? Grandpa told her about how his own son had wanted to throw him out of the house, about what kind of wife he had. He told Liza that a girl like her born between June 15 and July 15 would "be cheerful, plump, suffer a great deal of shame from various slanders, and, once married, have strange dreams . . ." In short, Liza made Grandpa's life fuller and more animated.

Liza's life, however, soon came to resemble ours. Mama took to her at first but soon grew angry at the girl's whims. Finally, after accidentally spilling Mama's snuffbox, she received a blow and learned that her benefactresses' touch was not always so light. After that, the orphan was completely lost in the crowd of children and Mama forgot about her existence. She didn't have her own pillow or blanket, and her dress was in tatters. We gave her our rags and sewed her an apron from scraps of different colors. The girl's benefactress did not notice that it was time to cover up her ward's nakedness. When reminded of this, Mama replied angrily, "As if I don't have enough of my own! She managed before; why does she suddenly need so much?"

Aunt Alexandra Semyonovna repurposed her old shirts and dresses. She also placated Mama. Having begged some scrap from her, our aunt made Mama believe that she herself had thought to give it to Liza. On these occasions, the girl could not help but look at her benefactress with horror. Upon hearing her footsteps—and Mama's gait resembled the commander's in *Don Juan*—the pale, trembling orphan hid behind our skirts, the chest of drawers, or wherever she could find. Most often, she ran to Grandpa, whom Mama never noticed. At the sight of Mama, the doll fell from her hands, the food stuck in her throat, and she looked at us so plaintively, as if asking for protection. But she needn't have feared: Mama gave orders to our aunt, scolded us, and left without even casting a glance at the frightened creature who was so indebted to her beneficence.

Soon the family's population began to decline. Misha rarely came home from his teacher. He had grown up and became handsome. Sixteen years old, he was tall and broad-shouldered and could pass for eighteen. He was swarthy, with eyes as black as coal, unusually thick and long eyelashes, and surprisingly beautiful eyebrows. His wavy black hair, always in a state of disarray, gave him a brave and rugged look. His teeth, his mouth—everything about him was surprisingly attractive, except for his perpetually serious, even gloomy expression and rigid manner. He took after our father, who apparently fostered something like love for him, punishing him more harshly and talking to him more often.

Once, when Misha had not visited us for a month, he suddenly appeared, out of breath, pale and agitated. He announced to Aunt Alexandra Semyonovna that he had run away from his teacher, who had wanted to punish him.

"I've decided to go to the Caucasus," he said, "and I came to ask Father and Mother . . ."

Auntie burst into tears and begged him, "Misha, what are you doing here? Your father will give you a flogging; go back."

"No, if you please! I'm not afraid of a beating. I'm going to the Caucasus no matter what!"

And he went straight to the drawing room.

Mama was dozing on the sofa, waiting for Kirilo Kirilych and other guests; the card table was ready. When she saw her son, she jumped up and asked menacingly, "What is it? What are you doing here?"

"I came on business," my brother answered in a firm voice.

"What! How do you . . . ?" Mama rose majestically from the sofa and made toward Misha, but he motioned her to be seated and approached her himself. She was taken aback by his audacity but soon came to her senses and asked, "What do you want?"

"I want to go to the Caucasus. I've come to ask permission from you and Father."

"The Caucasus! You little snot, I'll give you a thrashing!"

"Kill me if you like, but I am going to the Caucasus! Didn't you yourself reproach me for being a lazy good-for-nothing? Didn't you say my mother and father are ruining themselves to provide for me? Now I will save you the expense!"

Mama could not believe her ears (she thought she had taught her children obedience) and went silent for a moment. At last, she said sarcastically, "Very well! Go, I'll tell your father."

But our brother stood still. Astonished, Mama shouted, "I'm telling you to go!"

"I'll go. . . . Don't shout. . . . Just let me stay until Father gets up, otherwise God only knows what you'll tell him!"

"You're mad! You're drunk! I'll have you kicked out of the house!" our mother shouted.

"I'll leave when I want to!" Misha cried ferociously, but when he saw our pale-faced father appeal at the door, he became flustered and left off. Noticing her husband, Mama burst into tears and told him everything with various additions, finally announcing that Misha had been rude to her.

"I wasn't rude to you, Mother," Misha said.

"Do you hear, Andrei? He's a good-for-nothing drunk!"

"Shut up!" Father said angrily. He sat down at the card table. Mama quieted down and fixed her eyes on him. Father tightened his lips strangely.

"Why did you leave your teacher?" he asked his son sternly.

Misha hesitated.

"Well, tell me!" And Father turned even paler.

"I want to go to the Caucasus," said Misha timidly.

Father frowned. He clenched an unopened deck of cards lying on the table, and the cards broke free with a plaintive retort. He asked in a hollow voice, "Is it really so bad living with your father and mother?"

"No, sir. . . . But Mama reproaches me for everything . . ."

"Do you hear, Andrei?"

"Will you shut up?" Father shouted at her. He threw down the crumpled cards, which scattered on the table and were painfully bent, now freed from his grip. Mama, looking at the cards with compassion, raised her eyes to the ceiling and moved her lips as if in prayer.

"Why are you so lazy?" Father asked Misha.

"I'm not lazy, Papa. . . . I just want to serve in the Caucasus. . . . Mama keeps scolding me. . . . She won't even buy me boots . . ."

"Hm!" said Father. His face changed. Even Mama didn't dare be offended by her son's remark. She looked at her husband silently.

"Well, and what if I don't let you go to the Caucasus, and force you to study. . . . Eh?"

Misha looked down silently.

"I asked you a question!" said Father, the familiar signs of rage appearing more clearly on his face: his eyes were bloodshot; his lips had turned blue. Trembling, he rose slightly from his chair. His gaze seemed to burn Misha, who answered quietly and hesitantly, "I don't want to study. I'm going to the Caucasus."

"Don't *want* to?" asked Father in a voice that made Misha go pale. But, as if he'd decided on a desperate act, Misha finally looked at Father and said firmly, "No!"

We stood by the door breathlessly; I was ready to throw myself at my brother's feet and beg him to say "Yes." But I didn't have the strength to move: Father's face was so terrifying. Mama listened to their conversation intently, and when Misha challenged Father so recklessly, she involuntarily cried out, "Ah!"

Misha, who had been standing with his head bowed, now proudly straightened up and looked straight at Father's pale and sullen face, as if wanting to read his fate on it. This oppressive silence lasted for several minutes. Father was the one to break it, getting up from the table and saying to his son, "Let's go to my study. We'll talk there."

Misha followed him with a firm gait.

We recoiled from the door in horror. Aunt Alexandra Semyonovna cried so hard for her nephew, whom she loved very much and spoiled most of all. Father locked the office from the inside: How were we to know what they were saying? I rushed to Grandpa, whose room was next to the study: maybe we could hear from there. When I entered his room, I saw him on his knees in the corner. Pale and trembling, he stretched his arms out to the icon, then clamped his ears and whispered, gasping for breath, "My God . . . my God! . . . He'll kill him! His own son. Lord, don't let him . . ."

Grandpa fell backward. At first, I didn't understand what had happened to him, but suddenly the familiar sound of a long whip struck my ear. The blows slowly followed one after another with a hissing and screeching noise. Each was accompanied by a short question from Father. But there was no voice, not a word or sound in response—a deep silence behind the wall, as if the blows and questions were not directed toward a living being. I was beginning to think that Father was alone in the office talking to himself. . . . But suddenly I heard a faint, agonizing moan, and soon the moans resounded more clearly after each blow. There was no longer any doubt that it was my brother! I looked with horror at Grandpa, who had already lost the ability to speak and was only pointing at the study door. I rushed to Aunt Alexandra Semyonovna in tears and told her everything; she made for the study but ran into Misha at the door. His face was pale and distorted, and he shook as though feverish. His face was slightly swollen and twitching convulsively, and his breathing was unsteady and heavy. We were all silent, not daring to ask him what had happened. He took his cap, shot us a mocking look, and said, "Goodbye, I'm going to the Caucasus." Then he left. Aunt Alexandra Semyonovna ran after him, but he had already disappeared.

From that day on, Misha was hardly ever at home. Our aunt took to her bed, and Father, convinced that it was impossible to break his son's stubbornness, agreed to his departure. Misha was in a hurry to receive his junker greatcoat and spoke of nothing but the Caucasus. Father started visiting the nursery to talk with him about the Caucasus and about shooting, a skill my brother had mastered. Our mother was very angry with Father for showing weakness and thus encouraging the children toward disobedience. Father knew a colonel who was on his way to the Caucasus and had agreed to take our brother with him.

The day of departure finally arrived. The worries and tears started that morning: I cried, but secretly I envied my brother that he was leaving our parents' house. It came time to say farewell. Mama called for her son and sat alone with him for a long time. When Misha returned to the nursery, we asked him what she had said. He answered, "She's singing a different tune, but it's too late now."

Grandpa walked around the nursery glumly and kept groaning about how it was possible to send "such a pretty picture" to the Caucasus: some monster of a Circassian would kill or mutilate him. Father was also gloomy—he kept talking to the colonel. Father was seeing them off and kept hurrying them to say their goodbyes as quickly as possible. At last, the horses were ready. Everyone rushed into the hall, and our ailing aunt was practically carried in and placed on the sofa. Mama ordered everyone to sit down, and we did. There was a heavy silence.

She rose, and everyone stood up after her.[1] Breaking down in tears, she took the icon, blessed her son with it, kissed him on the forehead, and said tragically, "God be with you! May your mother's blessing be upon you wherever you go!"

Then, turning to the colonel, she asked him to look after her son and told him how it pains a mother's heart to let her child go so far away. Father cut her off with annoyance. He did not say goodbye to his son but kept hurrying others and repeatedly saying, "Come, it's time to go . . ." Grandpa, still groaning, kissed his grandson and quietly slipped a white banknote into his hand, whispering tearfully, "Here, Misha, for tobacco!"

"Goodbye, Grandpa, thank you."

My brother grew pale when he turned to our aunt. She trembled and let out a faint cry. Misha wanted to finish the farewell as soon as possible, but Alexandra Semyonovna embraced her beloved nephew with her weak arms and, kissing him, said in a tearful voice, "Misha. . . . Take care of yourself. . . . Don't forget us . . ."

Turning even paler, Father said angrily, "Come on, Sasha, it's time for him to go."

Sobbing, Auntie released her tearful nephew, who then bade farewell to us: "Goodbye, Fedya. . . . Goodbye, Sonya. . . . Goodbye, Tanya . . ." The smacking of kisses and the sounds of suppressed sobs resounded in the hall. "Goodbye, Misha," I said, pressing my lips firmly to my brother's pale cheeks. "Goodbye, Natasha . . ." Sobbing, I reached into my apron pocket and took out a pouch of my needlework, sewn from scraps, and presented it to my brother, who said, "Thanks, now I'll have two. Well, goodbye, goodbye, goodbye . . ." And for a long time that "goodbye" sounded in my ears, weighing on me so heavily that I wanted to smash my head against the wall.

We accompanied Misha to the carriage. As he and the colonel got settled, I remembered our sick aunt left alone in the hall, too weak to go downstairs, and I rushed to her. She was looking longingly at the door, but when she saw me, she brightened and asked anxiously, "Has he left?"

"Not yet."

I brought the sick patient to the window.

"Soon?" she asked, breathing weakly.

"Yes, they're going now. Ah, there he is!"

The carriage drove out the gate and sped past the windows. I bowed and waved to my brother. He saw us and waved back. Auntie stared at him with all her strength, and when the carriage disappeared, she staggered and fell into a chair. Her lips were pale, her eyes rolled, and she fainted.

Chapter Nine

MAMA MUST HAVE BEEN very upset by her son's departure; she remembered him every time she scolded our brothers: "Just you try signing up to go off to the Caucasus, I'll settle things without your father!" Uncle Semyon announced that it was time to send Fyodor to an institute.

"Oh, how wonderful," she exclaimed angrily. "Just when I send one away, it's time to think about the other! Why don't I just send them all to the Caucasus at once?"

Fyodor had managed to survive our uncle, who was so addicted to cards that he came to our house every day to play grand solitaire in the mornings. If the cards were in his favor, he smugly rubbed his hands and walked around the room deep in thought. If not, he went back to bed—as if the day had never dawned! Grandma had cried at her grandson's departure, but Fyodor rejoiced that he had finally escaped his uncle. For a long time afterward my brother's face would always change at the sight of him.

Grandma was so accustomed to quarreling with Grandpa that she had grown bored in her new life, and out of grief had doubled her portion of wine.

"What kind of life is this!" she told us. "I don't have anyone to talk to. When Fedya was there, it was fine! But now? Semyon sleeps like a dead man, and I sit there all by myself. Believe it or not, I have trouble eating: Pyotr Akimych used to shout at me, but at least he was a living person, someone to trade a few words with. God knows we lived together a long time—that's nothing to sniff at!" And she washed her tears down with tea. To console her, we described Grandpa's lifestyle and various eccentricities.

"Is he sleeping, Vanya?" Grandma asked.

"No, ma'am, just lying there. Would you like to look at him? I'll go to his room and leave the door open behind me."

"All right, go."

Through the crack in the door, Grandma peered at her husband who, grinding his teeth, lay motionless on the bed as if in a coffin. She was sad to see that he had lost a good deal of weight, although this was impossible, since he was nothing but skin and bones to begin with. Vanya delighted Grandma by informing the old man that his spendthrift wife had paid a visit. Grandpa jumped up, looked at the door, and whispered, "Look at how she's dolled herself up, Vanyusha! Your old granny's ready for a ball, and, you know, that's nothing compared to when she was young!"

"Grandpa!" said Ivan.

"What?"

"Do you know the senator who lives below us?"

"I've seen him around. . . . What about him?"

"Well, he stopped me on the stairs and asked me to inquire about Grandma. . . . 'It's a pity,' he said, 'that she has a husband, otherwise I'd marry her now!' But, after all, with his rank, perhaps he'll petition, and you'll get divorced."

"And where did he lay his eyes on her?" asked Grandpa, alarmed.

"What do you mean? They always see each other at the gate. He makes way for her and bows."

"Ah, so he's got it in his head to marry her! I may not live happily with the woman, but I will not grant her a divorce!" Grandpa was getting hot and banging his fist on the table. "To tell you the truth, I've thought it for a long time: she's not getting all dolled up for no reason! Not for nothing do they say, 'devout on the outside, love-sick in the inside . . .'"

A minute later Grandpa appeared in the nursery with a snuffed candle, supposedly in search of a light. He approached the tea table where Grandma was sitting, pretended to be surprised, and said, "Oh, I didn't know you were here! Good day, Nastasya Kirillovna . . ."

Then, mockingly, he bowed low to his wife. She rose from her chair seriously and responded with a similar bow, saying, "Good day to you, Pyotr Akimych!"

"How is your health?"

"God be thanked, Pyotr Akimych, and yours?"

"What, my health? My own son threw me out . . ." And he forced his wife to listen to his long story, in which she herself played a large role.

"That's enough out of you, Pyotr! Aren't you ashamed to dredge up the past?"

"And, in your opinion, I suppose, I ought to forget it all? I know everything! Even though we live apart you can't fool me!" He shook his finger at his wife. "I don't care if he's a senator! I spit on him!" And he spat . . .

"What are you on about now? What senator?"

"Oh, you really don't know? Come now, don't even dream of it! A divorce? I don't want one! We lived together for thirty years, and if it weren't for our scoundrel of a son . . ."

Embarrassed by this troubling memory, Grandpa clutched his head. With a wild cry, he ran to his room, where he continued sending threats to the senator who dared to fall in love with his wife.

Sometimes Grandpa invited Grandma over to our house. They were served tea and did not empty their cups quickly—Grandpa diligently topped them off with rum. The spouses' faces assumed a pleasant expression, and their conversation consisted of the transfer of mutual suffering. But Grandpa could not do without referencing the calendar, which Grandma could not stand. A quarrel would break out, and Grandma would run out, calling her husband a grouch and a miser. Grandpa followed her, shouting, "I know everything! You can't catch old birds with chaff! Woman is a fool! Spendthrift!"

We hurried to separate them. For the next two weeks, Grandpa would not stop talking for a minute about the latest quarrel, inviting everyone to weigh in.

Summer came. Mama decided to rent a dacha, supposedly for our ill aunt. The idea probably came to her from the doctors who had advised Kirilo Kirillovich to take the summer air and bathe in the sea. We were left in the city under Aunt Stepanida Petrovna's supervision. Our father, busy with his work and billiards, was hardly at home and went to the country very rarely. He was not at all surprised by Mama's tender attention to Kirilo Kirilych: she managed to convince her husband that in this, as in everything, she had the children's best interests at heart.

"Andrei, do you really think it's so easy for me to bear the whims of Kirilo Kirilych? I put up with everything for the sake of the children, and how do they thank me?" Sighing, she continued, "Sometimes, when I have an unexpected expense, four hundred rubles for Pyotr or for Fyodor, I go straight to him, and he gives it to me. Well, we'll pay him back later, but, still, he's someone you can really turn to in need."

"I really don't know, Masha. It seems that we earn over a thousand rubles a month, and from lessons . . ."

"Well, obviously you don't know how much the children cost! For your daughters alone . . ." And Mama unfolded an endless chain of expenses for clothing, shoes, and the upbringing of his children.

"I'm also thinking about the future," she continued in a mysterious tone. "You know, Kirilo Kirilych has money, and he doesn't love his stepmother. Where will his money go when he dies? He has no relatives, and, God be thanked, we've known him for ten years. He's so thin and sickly. The doctor himself told me that he won't live long . . ."

Father never responded to his wife's calculations—whether he agreed with them or not, he alone knows. But Mama always took his silence as a sign of consent and acted at her discretion.

Our brothers came home for the summer holidays, but they were hardly around, no matter how much Stepanida Petrovna threatened to complain to our father, no matter how much I begged them. They always said, "What is there for us to do at home? We'll suffocate from the heat!" Secretly, I agreed with them. If I could have, I would have gladly run away to the gardens to breathe in clean air and look at the greenery. After that, let them punish me: punishment can be endured after such pleasure! My sisters withstood the heat and stuffiness more patiently than I did. Of course, the eldest had other things to think about: she was still being courted by Yakov Mikhailovich. He was a friend of Kirilo Kirilych and, therefore, enjoyed the friendship of our mother, who treated him with an air of patronage. Yakov Mikhailovich did errands for her and wrote out her letters and business papers. Kirilo Kirilych's favor for the young man was not without calculation, either: it was not so striking that he visited us every day when Yakov Mikhailovich did, too. After Mama left for the dacha, he practically settled in our nursery. Unfortunately for us, Kirilo Kirilych grew bored at our house without the usual guests, and Mama quickly returned from the dacha.

The next summer, to our great surprise, one morning Mama scolded us and told us to get dressed: we were going to the dacha! The carriage was brought around, and we began piling into it: me, Stepanida Petrovna, my two sisters, our little brother Ivan (our other brothers had not yet been dismissed for the holidays), and Aunt Alexandra Semyonovna, each of us with our own bundle. I could hardly breathe, so cramped was I and so happy at the prospect of seeing open fields and the sea. Luckily, I was pressed against the window. The thin suburban grass seemed incredibly luxurious to me, and the endless blue distance brought me such delight that I almost jumped out of the window, greedily gulping the not-quite-clean air, which nevertheless seemed aromatic.

"Can't you sit still? Watch it, you're squishing the bundle!" Mama shouted. Frightened and squeezed between the bundles and my sisters, I could not move my arms or legs, but my eyes ran along the path greedily and briskly. When I saw a field thick with golden chicory, I inadvertently gasped, "Oh, look how many flowers! Look, Katya!"

Mama asked angrily, "What is it?"

I did not dare make her a participant in my joy. I kept silent.

"I'm asking you, what is it?" she repeated.

"Flowers," I answered timidly, nodding toward the field, since my hands were occupied.

Mama glanced at the field and said, "Fool, in raptures over flowers . . ."

As we drove farther from the city, the surroundings became more and more beautiful. Not daring to speak, I nudged Katya and nodded toward the constantly changing objects of my surprise and delight.

I was watching the road so carefully that my head began spinning.

"Oh, Katya, are we going backward?" I asked in fright.

"What are you talking about? We just passed that cart!"

Once I calmed down, I started looking forward to seeing the dacha. I imagined it would be surrounded by a forest with bunches of flowers and berries, with the sea at our very windows. . . . We drove through the gate, and Mama said, "Thank

God, we're almost there." I was very surprised to see houses that looked like the ones in Saint Petersburg, only smaller; I saw only the occasional tree. We drove up to a low two-story house with a small shop on the ground floor. I thought Mama wanted to buy something there when she shouted to the coachman, "Stop, stop! The shop!" But when she added, "Well, someone get out!" I did a double take and couldn't believe my ears.

"So this is what you call a dacha!" I said in despair, looking around the miserable house and the dirty yard, littered with boards, logs, and construction waste. I nearly started crying. Running upstairs, I was even more surprised to see only two rooms: a small kitchen where you could barely turn around and another room, completely dark. That was all! So we'd have to sit with Mama all the time? A shiver ran down my spine . . .

"Auntie, are we really going to sleep in the same room as Mama?"

"No, we'll sleep in the dark room. Here we'll only drink tea and have dinner."

"What! We're going to eat dinner with her?"

Annoyed, I began to reproach my aunt for praising such a nasty dacha to us. She got angry and told me to hush: the partition was wooden, and Mama would hear us!

Angry and sad, I reluctantly joined my sisters, who were washing glasses and cups; only a cook, hired especially for this journey, was brought to the dacha with us. I don't know how, but a glass slipped out of my hands and broke with a crash. A second later, Mama was standing in front of me with her punishing hand, each blow accompanied by these words: "Fool! Always have been, always will be . . ."

At that moment, this kind of insult felt heavier than ever. I felt so humiliated that I barely refrained from revealing my indignation to my mother. In despair, I went into the hall, cried, and looked out the window, where I became distracted by movement in the distance. I peered out and saw an endless expanse of water that had completely merged with the sky. I opened the window and saw the sea even more clearly. Forgetting my grief, I looked at the smoke floating over the waves, the birds, flashing black spots in the mist, the small boats that disappeared completely and then reemerged. I really wanted to get a closer look, so I rushed to the yard, searching for a path to the sea . . . to no avail! The shopkeeper, who was calling his chickens, explained that I had to go through the city first, then go out onto the road, down the hill, and then I would reach the sea. . . . It was far. I convinced my sisters and Stepanida Petrovna, and we set off, with me as our guide. After passing the dachas, we saw a forest on the other side of the road and rushed to it: no flowers or berries, only sand and bare trees! On the other side of the forest there was a steep hill. I ran to it without thinking, leaving my sisters below. I was out of breath, unaccustomed as I was to such feats of strength, but I forgot my fatigue, struck by the view that opened up before me.

The sunlight played on the dark waves that rolled by, one after another. White sails flew like gigantic birds chasing after each other. The steamers left a white and patchy trail, in which broken, refracted rays of sun sparkled and glittered even more brightly. Sitting on top of the hill, I looked at the sea for a long time. The ceaseless movement of the waves made me sad. I remembered my brother Misha. Maybe just now, I thought, he's running through the mountains and hiding from Circassians. . . . I looked around and felt frightened to be alone. Rushing down the hill, I called out to my sisters. Fortunately, they were not sitting far away. I told them that you could see the sea from the hill and that the view of the forest was better there than from below. We climbed back up. After another glance at the sea, we descended and I risked running into the forest, though I called out to my sisters every minute. I returned home with a whole bunch of flowers. We were not greeted very kindly.

"And just where did you see fit to go off to?"

"The forest."

"The forest? Without asking? And you, Stepanida, you went, too, like a little girl!"

Stepanida Petrovna forgave her sister everything except hints at her maturity of years; a quarrel broke out.

The next day, after scolding us at tea, Mama decreed that we go swimming with her. I was given a mug and washcloth to carry, Katya a sheet, and Sonya a shirt. If we had tied everything into a bundle, there would have been a quarrel about who would carry it, so Auntie ordered us to do it this way.

We burned with shame as we walked through the streets. Many heads looked at us with strange curiosity from the windows of their dachas, and we heard their comments: "*Her* daughters . . . really? So poorly dressed. . . . I never would have thought . . ."

"Do you hear what they're saying about us?" I whispered, gently elbowing my sister. "How are we going to walk back?"

Suspecting nothing, Mama proudly forged on, accompanied by her daughters, who did not dare walk beside her: so majestic was she! We arrived at the swimming area in strict silence. By the way, none of the dacha residents, aside from our intrepid mother, went swimming at this spot so close to the road. Standing on tiptoe and stretching our arms up, we held a sheet in front of Mama while she undressed, but nevertheless . . . Mama let her hair down and plunged picturesquely into the waves. Watching her, I told my sisters that we were nymphs, and she was a goddess, and that we should turn into little fish and swim away from her. But the trouble with that: she might, after all, turn into a pike, overtake us, and swallow us whole. We joked on the shore while Mama dove under the waves. Then, she didn't come up for a long time. I was so scared that I almost threw myself into the water.

"Mama!" I screamed.

She poked her head out of the water. My shrill cry had reached her ears, and she shouted, "What are you yelling for?"

Her unexpected appearance and menacing voice frightened me even more. My sisters laughed at me, and my mother, whipping up foam around her, swam toward me like a sea monster. When she reached the shore and rose to her feet, I jumped back in panic. She repeated her question: "What are you yelling for?"

I was completely tongue-tied, and Mama's palm, wet from the sea, met my pale cheek. Perhaps for the first time since the creation of the world, there was a resounding blow on the seashore, and Echo repeated it several times, as if rejoicing at a new sound.

Our homeward procession was the same, with the very same remarks pursuing us from the windows.

CHAPTER NINE

The next day, I began to limp, and thereby attempted to avoid more caresses from my mother. My sisters were cross with me and annoyed that they had not thought of such an excuse to miss swimming. Sometimes in the evening Mama took us for a walk in the gardens, where music was playing. On these occasions, God knows why, I completely lost control of myself and knocked into almost everyone I crossed paths with. Hurrying to regain composure and make it past each other, the stranger and I would shift in a frenzy from side to side, until Mama's menacing voice turned me to stone. Then the weary gentleman would apologize to me, and Mama would tell the whole street how appalled she was to have such a fool of a daughter: you couldn't take her anywhere! When we passed ladies all dressed up, I glanced around at myself and my sisters. We were always dressed the same as each other, probably so as not to inspire envy among us. This tactic carried another advantage: from three worn-out dresses, we could always stitch together a completely new one. We had no gloves and wore thin shoes of the poorest quality. Our clothing completed our misfortune, drawing the public's attention to us, with our gaudy identical hats and identical cotton cloaks, while everyone else simply wore dresses in the unbearable heat.

Fortunately, Mama did not really enjoy these walks. Most often we spent the day huddled away from the heat in the dark room. Although even there we had cheerful moments and laughed heartily.

Once Mama spent three days fretting over some sort of pâté, and before dinner she ordered us not to touch it even if it was offered to us. The pâté was served. Solemnly standing up and cutting off a piece with the skill of a surgeon, she handed a plate to Kirilo Kirilych. He was incredibly polite and sometimes, to the annoyance of our mother, even showed kindness to my sisters and Stepanida Petrovna, who lured him with flattery. Taking the plate, Kirilo Kirilych very tactfully offered it to me. I refused.

"Well, then, can I trouble you to pass it to Stepanida Petrovna?"

The plate began its journey around the table. When it passed Ivan's nose, our brother enthusiastically inhaled the smell and spoke loudly, shaking his head: "Oh, I couldn't. . . . I don't care for it, even the smell is dreadful."

Mama gloomily followed the peregrinations of the plate, and when it returned home she offered it again to Kirilo Kirilych. He flatly refused, complaining that he was not in good health that day.

"Well then, you all can help yourselves!" Mama shouted, shoving the plate into the middle of the table.

The effect was amazing. Mama got hold of herself, but it was too late—Kirilo Kirilych was put off. Immediately after dinner he said, "Goodbye, Marya Petrovna."

"Where are you going? What about coffee?"

"I want to go to sleep," he answered dryly.

"As you wish."

Stepanida Petrovna and my sisters were waiting in the hall to detain him, to spite our mother. I stayed in the dining room to watch how she would react to their talk and laughter.

"Who's there?" she asked me.

"I don't know, ma'am!"

"Go look, and tell your sisters to stop chattering!"

I repeated her message word for word, hoping to harden Kirilo Kirilych against her even more. Sure enough, he started laughing and talking even louder. Mama was upset; the talking and laughter tormented her. Finally, she walked to the door with steps that made the wooden house tremble. Opening the door noisily, she shouted with rage, "Who's making all this racket? Oh, you're still here," she added meekly, pretending to be surprised. Then she turned to Stepanida Petrovna: "Can't you quiet them down. . . . Just look how you're riling them up—you know better! Kindly take them to their room!"

This is how we spent two weeks at the dacha. Upon returning to the city, the nursery seemed like paradise to us. Soon after, a letter arrived from the Caucasus. To our surprise, Father brought it to the nursery himself and gave it to Aunt Alexandra Semyonovna to read. She cried with joy. Father teased her and spoke cheerfully: "Hey, what are you crying for? Soon your nephew will be an officer."

We read the letter: the colonel informed us that Misha had shown spectacular bravery, had already received the Cross of St. George, and was already being put up for officer. At the end of his letter, the colonel advised Father to bring Misha back from the Caucasus as soon as he was made an officer because with his hot head he ought not to remain there much longer. The nursery filled with joyful chatter; we were already counting the days until our brother came home to us. Vanya conveyed the news to Grandpa in his own special way: "Misha killed twenty-five Circassians."

Grandpa turned pale and dismissed him with a wave.

"Stop it, Vanyusha."

"It's true, Grandpa."

"Well, how would he have killed them?"

Ivan made his hand into a gun, aimed at Grandpa, and shouted, "Bang!" Grandpa clutched his chest as if a bullet had struck him. Ivan laughed. Grandpa got angry and went to bother others with questions about his grandson.

Exactly two months later, the postman came with another letter from the colonel. We joyfully brought the letter to Father, returned to the nursery, and, gathering in a bunch, waited impatiently: our father would come and announce that Misha had been made an officer. . . . But time passed, and Father did not come. Tired of waiting, we quietly approached his study. The door was locked, and there was silence. Evening came. We decided that we would probably get to hear the letter tomorrow. Tea was served. Auntie went to the study and knocked on the door.

"Who's there?" Father said faintly.

"Me, brother. Would you like some tea?"

"No!"

Auntie concluded that Father had quarreled with Mama, and she became worried. We went to bed. Auntie went to the study three times, and in the morning said that she was frightened. The light in the study had not been put out that night, and she heard moaning from time to time.

Father came to the nursery while Mama was still sleeping. We hardly recognized him: his face was terribly pale, his eyes swollen, and he even seemed thinner—he looked pitiful. Kissing his hand, I noticed it was shaking. Father hesitated strangely and finally let out a heavy sigh. Stammering, and not looking at anyone, he said, "Your brother has been killed. . . . Don't talk about him anymore, and don't tell your mother . . ." And he hurried out.

The nursery filled with sobs. Aunt Alexandra Semyonovna was a terrible sight. Fortunately, Mama did not notice our tear-stained faces, and she was already used to seeing Auntie sick and sad. Father was still sitting in the study. He didn't have dinner, and by evening he had dressed and left.

We rushed into the study, and I was the first to grab the letter from the table: it was all rippled, and the ink was so blurred that many words were impossible to make out. I was able to read a few phrases: "He died without much suffering . . . the bullet hit him right in the heart . . . he was a brave fellow, but with his character, at his age, he should not have been put in such danger . . ." A few more consolations, and we couldn't make out the rest. I had barely put the letter back in its original place when Father returned. He went into the drawing room, where they were already playing cards. Noticing his thinness and pallor, Mama asked, "What's wrong with you, Andrei?"

He sat down on the sofa without answering. Mama continued dealing. He told her quietly, "I received a letter from the Caucasus yesterday."

"Well, what did it say?" she asked, sorting her cards by suit.

"Misha," he began. "Misha's been . . . wounded."

He stood up to hide his distress.

"Badly or not?" Mama asked quickly.

Father hesitated. The game stopped. Mama looked intently at her husband and screamed shrilly, "Oh! He's been killed!"

The cards fell out of her hand, and she collapsed on the sofa in terrible convulsions. Father went to her. He was shaking all over, and for the first and last time in my life I saw tears streaming down my father's pale face.

Chapter Ten

SOON THE SHUFFLING OF CARDS was heard again in the drawing room.

Learning of his grandson's death, Grandpa cried and reproached our parents for letting "such a pretty picture" go to the Caucasus. Grandma came running to us, crying, and asked about every last detail.

"Oh, my God! It would be better if your old grandmother had died. . . . What good is my life? And I set aside ten rubles for him: I thought my grandson the officer was coming home. So much for Misha! There is nothing worse than dreaming of a tooth falling out! I dreamed that the other day! That's not a good sign, I thought! I went to the Savior on Haymarket and lit a candle . . ."[1]

Uncle took the news indifferently, only saying, "If they'd sent him to me, I'd have schooled him, all right. He'd have forgotten all about the Caucasus . . ."

After a while, no one spoke of Misha. Only sometimes I dreamed that he was alive and I was glad. We would talk, but then suddenly he would turn pale and leave me, saying, "Time to go to the grave." Then I would stare intently at his face, but instead of my brother I'd be looking at a hideous dead man.

Sonya was clearly interested in Yakov Mikhailovich—once I happened to see them holding hands. He showered my sister with various pleasantries, but she treated him rather cruelly. Often in his presence she would admire some officer she had happened to see, while poor Yakov Mikhailovich sat on pins and needles. Stepanida Petrovna would pester him with intimate questions: Why was he in such poor spirits? He took out his anger on her by giving rude answers. They quarreled, and sometimes he would not appear again in the nursery for two days. Then Stepanida Petrovna would cry softly. Mama continued to tolerate his presence in our house, if only for his services as her clerk and messenger. She did not fear for her daughters: he was poor and ugly. But apparently Mama's patience had its limits. When Yakov Mikhailovich left his post due to some unpleasant business, Mama abruptly changed her treatment of him: he had become all too insignificant. Poor Yakov Mikhailovich endured her insults heroically: love gave him strength. Finally, one day he entered the nursery very pale and choking with anger. Stepanida Petrovna pestered him with questions, but he did not reply and soon took his leave. The next evening, he appeared in the drawing room very sad and announced that he was moving to a distant province for three years.

Stepanida Petrovna assumed that this sacrifice was on her account: clearly, he wanted to improve his affairs in order to get married! Indeed, it seemed so, only he did not intend to marry her. His farewell with my sister was touching. I felt sorry for him: he could not look at my her without crying. I happened to overhear their conversation.

"Will you forget me, Sofia Andreevna?"

"Why would I forget you?"

"Promise me again: When I come back, will I find you just as kind as you are now?"

Stepanida Petrovna dashed over to him with a pencil and asked for his address.

Yakov Mikhailovich replied that he would write to us first, and that now it was time for him to go.

"Goodbye, Sofia Andreevna, don't forget . . ."

His emotion prevented him from finishing. Stepanida Petrovna pestered him with requests to write often. He began his farewells exactly five times. Finally, in despair, he went up to Sofia, kissed her hand firmly and slowly, and then suddenly pressed his pale lips to her rosy cheek. Flustered, Sonya cried, "Yakov Mikhailovich!" Stepanida Petrovna readied herself for her own goodbye kiss, but Yakov Mikhailovich had already run out of the nursery. She flew into a rage.

We were more bored than ever at home. Before, Yakov Mikhailovich had enlivened our nursery by reading aloud and telling us about the news. I especially loved when he read to us: I could have listened to those novels all night.

A month later we received a letter from Yakov Mikhailovich. The next morning, on my way to the music teacher, an unknown gentleman handed me another letter to give to my sister and disappeared. My sister was completely unsurprised to receive the letter: she must have known in advance who it was from.

"Sonya, is it from Yakov Mikhailovich?"

"Yes, but I'm afraid Auntie will find out, and she will certainly tell Mama. . . . Tomorrow give it back and don't accept any more letters."

"So you don't love him, Sonya?" I asked in surprise.

"No; he had the idea I would marry him."

"Why don't you want to marry him? You let him hold your hand!"

"So what if I did? Now I don't want to, so do me a favor and don't accept any more letters."

With no other choice, the next day I fearfully returned the letter to the stranger, whom I found standing in the same place. My sister began attending church more often and started talking about some blue eyes she saw there.

A month passed. Once again on my way to the music teacher, I saw the same gentleman with another letter. I refused it, but he shoved it into my hand and disappeared.

Sonya was angry and ordered me to return the letter the next day with a small note of her own, which she wrote right then and there. I complied.

After that, I never saw the strange gentleman again.

Yakov Mikhailovich informed our aunt that he intended to remain in the service in that province forever and stopped writing.

I asked Sonya whether she felt sorry for Yakov Mikhailovich. She told me that she had loved him because she had never known anyone else but that now she didn't care—it was for the best that he stayed in the province.

Stepanida Petrovna cheered up quickly, as well. By that time, her younger sister had graduated from one of the state schools. We loved this aunt: she wasn't smart, but she was kind and not bad looking. Stepanida Petrovna, who had lost all hope of marrying, wanted to at least marry off her younger sister so that she could move in with her and wound our pride—we were the same age as our young aunt. She was being courted by the son of an important man, in whose good graces Mama was hoping to land. Mama began inviting this son and her own younger sister over every day. Little by little, our parlor, previously almost empty, became a gathering place for young men and my sisters and aunts. Their chatter and laughter floated into the nursery, where I sat alone.

I didn't like sitting in the drawing room. I had begun to notice some changes in myself: sometimes I felt like crying for no reason, and other times I felt so merry that I jumped and ran like a child, even though I was already sixteen years old.

From time to time, I would sit for two hours at the window in total idleness. I watched the clouds, thinking about God knows what, and recalled novels that Yakov Mikhailovich had read, imagining myself as the heroine of one of them. . . . I enjoyed this strange state so much that I looked forward to the sunset, when the sky started getting dark. I would take a book, sit by the window, and pretend that I was studying. Meanwhile, I'd forget myself and where I was sitting—I'd forget everything and everyone. I imagined that I, too, was beneath the clouds, that I was struggling to break through them and then flying with incredible speed through the clear sky. Sometimes the clouds resembled various monsters I had heard about in fairy tales. And I was glad when a hostile cloud met another and, after a long struggle, completely disappeared. And how cross I was on completely dark evenings!

Stepanida Petrovna hated me, and when she noticed my behavior, she asked suspiciously, "What are you doing at the window? Can you even see anything at this hour?"

"I want to sit here! Why do you need to know everything?"

"Are you looking at the officers over there?"

There were officers living across from us, but I didn't pay attention to them; I still considered myself a child, and, besides, according to Stepanida Petrovna, I couldn't hope to attract anyone. However, her remark annoyed me. I answered sharply, "I still have years of officer-ogling ahead of me, but for you, I'm afraid, that time has come and gone!"

Enraged, she reminded me that I was ugly and stupid, that no one wanted to look at me, so I shouldn't even dream of getting married.

"I'm not thinking about it. . . . And if you're so clever, why has no one ever married you? Not even when you were younger?"

Hating me even more, she began following my every step, purposely misinterpreting my every word, and constantly finding fault with me. She managed to turn Aunt Alexandra Semyonovna against me, telling her that I was winking at passersby on my way to music lessons and that the teacher's wife told her that I was not practicing, only staring out the window all the time.

As soon as I went to the window, Alexandra Semyonovna also started spying on me. Frustrated, I abandoned my innocent observations and sat with my back to the window.

"Why don't you go to the parlor like your sisters? Why are you sitting alone at the window?" Alexandra Semyonovna asked me every evening when the guests came.

"What am I going to do there? It's boring for me, I don't understand what they talk about!"

After the guests left, our young aunt told my sisters about how the son of the important man was courting her. My sisters also whispered in secret. Only Stepanida Petrovna had nothing to recount or whisper about: no one was courting her.

One evening, I decided to go to the parlor. All the usual guests were there. In order to make his own frequent visits less obvious, the son of the important man would bring along three other young men whenever he called. One of them, Alexei Petrovich, asked me, "Why is it that I see you so rarely here?"

"I like to sit alone," I replied.

"Aren't you bored sitting alone? Well, what were you doing just now?"

I was ashamed to say that I had been watching the clouds, and thoughtlessly answered, "Reading."

"And what were you reading?"

I was embarrassed by my lie. Apart from general history, grammar, and geography, I didn't have any books in my possession. Fortunately, I remembered *The Ice Palace*, which Yakov Mikhailovich had read to me and my sisters.[2]

"A novel," I said.

"Which one?"

"*The Ice Palace*."

"Do you like it?"

"Very much."

"Would you like me to bring you a Walter Scott novel?"

"Thank you, but I dare not. I must ask my aunt."

"What do you mean? You dare not read a novel without your Auntie's permission?" Alexei Petrovich smiled. "How old are you?"

"Sixteen."

"Do you like flowers?"

"Yes, very much."

"Allow me to bring you a bouquet tomorrow."

"Oh, no! I must ask . . ." But I didn't finish because Alexei Petrovich laughed again. Flushed with anger, I went to the nursery, where I railed against him to Alexandra Semyonovna for an entire hour. Later that evening, my sister asked me why Alexei Petrovich had laughed so much while talking to me.

Stepanida Petrovna interrupted, "Surely you must have said something stupid? He kept asking afterward: Why doesn't she come back to the parlor?"

"He's stupid himself, that's why he laughs so much. . . . I'll never speak to him again."

"He wouldn't talk to a fool like you."

"Well, apparently, he thinks you're not very clever, either: he didn't say a word to you when I was there."

"Listen to her! She must have heard what he was saying about her. He was joking, you can be sure of that. . . . And here you are, thinking you're a pretty girl!"

"No one calls you pretty, even as a joke!" I said.

The next day I deliberately went to the parlor to prove that, if I wanted to, I could also chat like the others. I don't know where my words came from, but I talked incessantly. Stepanida

Petrovna kept sending me to bed, reminding me of my music lessons early the next day.

"What time do you leave for your lessons?" Alexei Petrovich asked me.

"Nine."

"Tomorrow I will also get up at nine and come to your teacher—we shall take lessons together."

"Please, don't do that," I began, frightened. . . . But then I stopped, embarrassed and blushing, when I noticed that same smile on his lips.

"You don't want me to?" he said. "Well, then, forbid me!"

"Why should I forbid you? You're not going to do it, anyway! If Sonya were taking lessons there, that would be another matter!"

"Why wouldn't I go to see you?" Alexei Petrovich asked quietly.

"Stepanida Petrovna told me you're in love with Sonya."

"Yes, I'm in love, but not with your sister," Alexei Petrovich said even more quietly, looking at me strangely.

Suddenly we both grew quiet. Alexei Petrovich's eyes burned my swarthy cheeks. I was red as a peony, breathing heavily and for some reason unable for the first time to look directly into his eyes. And my trepidation was increasing by the minute. I quietly said goodbye and ran away from the astonished Alexei Petrovich.

I didn't see him for a week, but I thought a lot about our conversation, remembering every word he said, sometimes even asking him questions and answering for him myself. Whenever I was convinced that he was being serious, suddenly I thought of the possibility that he was joking, and I did not dare return to the parlor.

I watched him through the crack of the door. He sat alone more often, and if he talked to my sisters or aunts, he seemed to do so reluctantly.

I even heard him ask, "Why doesn't your sister come out? Is she in good health?" My heart was beating so fast. When he found out that I was healthy, he seemed to frown.

No matter what I was doing, whenever I heard his name, I involuntarily stopped and shuddered.

Once during my lessons, I saw him drive past the teacher's house, and I almost fainted from fright. I imagined Mama and Stepanida Petrovna asking me why he was passing the teacher's house.

I began to stare at myself in the mirror: sometimes I thought that I was not as ugly and dark as Stepanida Petrovna said; then I found myself ugly again and almost cried from vexation.

Finally, I decided to return to the parlor. My heart was beating hard, and my voice trembled. Alexei Petrovich was very happy. He said, "Are you very cross with me? I'm sorry, I won't drive past your teacher's house anymore."

I relaxed and breathed more freely. I pretended that I didn't even know he had driven past.

"I didn't come to the parlor before simply because I didn't want to."

"Well, I wanted to see you very much," he said, sighing.

"Why?" I asked, blushing. He was silent, evidently finding it difficult to answer.

"I wanted to see you because I love your eyes!" And he looked intently at me.

I was always lost in such situations, but the fear of being deceived, of mistaking his joke for seriousness, quickly brought me to my senses. I asked, "Do you also love Stepanida Petrovna's eyes?"

"You're always making jokes!" He grew angry. I felt sorry for him and tried to cheer him up with various stories.

The next morning, envious that I was being paid attention, Stepanida Petrovna started a rumor that I had once more decided not to speak to Alexei Petrovich.

The following evening, I did indeed try to avoid speaking with him, which inadvertently interested him even more. My eyes shone more than usual, and even I felt some kind of power in them. While Stepanida Petrovna was gone, I managed to tell Alexei Petrovich about my position, and I felt better. Having confided my secret, I felt that something connected us. By the end of the evening, I had completely forgotten my promise and found myself talking to Alexei Petrovich again. While we stood at the piano, I leafed through a book and my hand accidentally touched his hand. He held it and squeezed it lightly. My head started spinning, the parlor disappeared, and I seemed to be swimming in air. When I came to, my hand was still in his, and he asked softly, "Do you love me?"

I answered automatically, "Yes," without knowing what I was saying.

"What are you doing here?" Stepanida Petrovna's voice rang out.

I shuddered. Alexei Petrovich was embarrassed.

"We are looking at sheet music," he told her angrily.

She smiled and walked away. Beside myself with happiness, I said goodbye to Alexei Petrovich and went to bed as soon as I could. It was only then that I realized the full extent of my recklessness. "What if he's playing a prank on me? Let's assume that he really does love me—what then? Do we get married?" The thought of it made me laugh. "Alexei Petrovich is a young man," I thought, "quite rich, with many relatives who probably wouldn't allow him to marry me. I'm a poor, ugly girl, as Stepanida Petrovna likes to say. . . . Could someone really love me? I'm just a girl . . ."

Thinking I was asleep, Stepanida Petrovna and her sister reasoned among themselves that Alexei Petrovich was leading me by the nose and that the other young man courting my older sister would not marry her, either.

Alexandra Semyonovna took great offense at their conclusion. Stepanida Petrovna announced that she would wait a little longer, then tell Mama everything and put a stop to the young people's visits. She thought this plan would force the son of the important man to ask for her sister's hand as soon as possible.

After hearing my aunts' conversation, I could not fall asleep for a long time. I wondered: What should I do? I couldn't bear to stop seeing Alexei Petrovich. And Mama? What would happen when they told her about me? In her anger, she would likely invent some sort of humiliation that I'd have to endure in front of him. He couldn't marry me—my aunts knew best. They said that I was flirting with him. Remembering some of my words and looks, I realized they were right. Then I felt unbearable agony, anguish, and shame. . . . What could I do? Run away from Alexei Petrovich, from Mama, from my aunts? Where could I go? They would find me and bring me back to my father and irate mother. I imagined my parents' angry faces when they received their runaway daughter. I was so frightened that I decided it was better to refuse to see Alexei Petrovich, to endure that suffering rather than incite my mother's wrath. "I'll tell him I don't love him!" And I started thinking, "How do I know I love him? Maybe it doesn't matter that time seems to move slowly when he's not around, that I can't think about anything but him, that I don't want to look at anyone but him? On the contrary, when I hear his voice, I sit up, my heart starts beating faster, and I feel so kindhearted that I'm ready to give my hand even to my enemy Stepanida Petrovna. I feel sad saying goodbye to him when I know I won't see him the next day. What will happen to me when I don't see him at all?" I hugged my pillow tightly and used it to stifle my sobs.

Chapter Eleven

THE NEXT DAY I woke up with reddened eyes.

"Were you crying about Alexei Petrovich?" Stepanida Petrovna asked.

"What's it to you? Leave me alone!" I said. My eyes welled up with tears again. Stepanida Petrovna spoke in a pitying voice: "Poor thing! She thought he was going to marry her! No, he won't marry you, even if you cry every day from morning 'til night," she concluded in a harsh voice that suited her face better.

After such a painful night, I did not have the patience to endure her ridicule. Holding my head in my hands, I leaned against the wall and sobbed. They scolded me for crying so loudly.

"If only I could run away!" I said in despair, not knowing what I was saying, and suddenly Stepanida Petrovna's hideous, triumphant laugh brought me to my senses.

"Is that so!" she hissed. "Oh my, Natalya! What a surprise you're cooking up for your parents! Running away with Alexei Petrovich? It's true, you've always had that look . . ."

At the name of Alexei Petrovich and such insulting suspicions, my tears dried. I went up to her, and I don't know where I found the words, but I did not leave her insults unanswered. I knew that her sister was at that time in the very position that she predicted for me.

Extremely irritated, Stepanida Petrovna vowed to tell my mother everything. And at dusk she went to see her.

The gathering storm, the fear that I would perhaps never see Alexei Petrovich again, the premonition of a fresh humiliation—all this inspired a brave thought. I decided at all costs to see Alexei Petrovich, to tell him everything, and bid him farewell forever.

I begged Ivan to go downstairs, wait for Alexei Petrovich to arrive, and ask him to wait for me there.

"Natasha, please don't! What if they see!?"

"If they see you, it's all right, and if they see me, I'd rather die than say you helped me."

"What do you want to tell him?"

I struggled to answer my brother's question.

"You'll run straight to Grandpa afterward," I said, once he agreed to my request. "That way I'll know Alexei Petrovich is waiting for me."

"Well, all right!"

The hour came when Alexei Petrovitch and the other guests usually arrived. I was so nervous. Suddenly Ivan ran noisily into

Grandpa's room. I almost gave myself away: I wanted so much to rush to the door at once. But I restrained myself, stood calmly, and went out into the front hall without hurrying. Then I ran down the stairs like an arrow, almost knocking down Alexei Petrovich, who was shivering from the cold. For a moment I was frightened I had bumped into someone else.

"Oh, how you startled me!" I said.

"What's the matter with you? Calm down! I know everything: your brother told me . . ."

I grew even more frightened, wondering whether my brother had told him about my quarrel with Stepanida Petrovna.

"Oh, what did he do? Don't listen to him: he likes to talk!"

"No, I know everything, and I beg you not to worry . . ." He took my hand. "Why are you trembling? Oh, my God! You've only got on a dress! You'll catch cold!" He wanted to cover me with his overcoat. I jumped back quickly.

"No, I'm warm. I must tell you everything as quickly as possible. Mama knows everything, she . . ."

"I'm telling you, I know everything, and—don't be afraid!" Then he continued in a voice that seemed solemn, "You must tell me honestly: Do you love me?" Alexei Petrovich took my hand and pulled me to him. The blood rushed to my head, and I said, "Yes, I love you."

"Very much?"

I caught myself and responded, "Do you want to know this so that you can make fun of me?"

"What do you mean?" said Alexei Petrovich in surprise, releasing my hand from his.

"Stepanida Petrovna keeps telling me . . ."

Alexei Petrovich grew cross. He wrapped himself tightly in his overcoat, then completely undid it, as if he were getting hot, and said to me, "Fine! Today I will prove to you just how much of a joke this is to me, and you'll be ashamed you believed the others."

I always liked it when he was cross: it seemed to me then that he loved me, and—now I don't understand how—I told him many times that I loved him very much. He asked permission to kiss me, but I firmly refused.

"Surely you will kiss me tomorrow as your bridegroom?" he said.

"My bridegroom! Do you really want to get married?"

"Didn't you say yourself that you love me?"

When Alexei Petrovich spoke to me quietly, I didn't know what I was doing. I was completely at his mercy. I don't know how it happened, but I felt his warm breath, and his hot lips touched my cheek. I did not resist. Tears welled up in my eyes; I burned all over, but it felt good.

Suddenly I heard a voice on the stairs: "Natasha!" My brother was standing in front of us. "Run quick! They're looking for you!"

In my fright I forgot everything and, seizing my brother by the hand, made to run, but Alexei Petrovich held me back.

"Wait," he pleaded.

"I'm afraid: my aunt is looking for me."

"Well, then, until tomorrow; don't forget what you said. And now I shall go speak to your mother."

"Oh, no, wait! They may guess; you'd better come in an hour!"

"Well, goodbye!"

And Alexei Petrovich kissed my hand. I felt a shiver, and some strange feeling took possession of me: as if, having had my hand kissed for the first time, I was no longer a little girl. Passing through the hall, where the dog was always lying tied to a chain, I thought, "Now the wicked dog will bark and let everyone know where I've been." But she was curled up, dozing, and at my appearance she only opened and closed her sleepy eyes and tapped her tail twice in greeting. I went into the nursery. It seemed to me that Alexei Petrovich's lips had left a fiery mark on my cheek. I covered it with my hand but felt it there still. I was so nervous. But I needn't have worried: my absence had gone unnoticed.

Exactly one hour later, the dog started barking. Stepanida Petrovna eagerly peered into the hallway and said with a triumphant smile, "Here's Alexei Petrovich."

But when she met my prideful and contemptuous gaze, she lost her nerve and hurriedly turned away.

I sat down in a corner and did not take my eyes off her: she was strangely embarrassed, turning around in her chair, then moving to another one. My eyes seemed to burn her conscience. Finally, she couldn't stand it anymore and asked, "What are you staring at?"

"I'm trying to read in your eyes how many lies and accusations you've told Mama today."

"Oh, my God! What's wrong with you? What impudence! Well, just wait, tomorrow you'll get what you deserve."

"We shall see!" I said so emphatically that she paled in surprise.

The guests dispersed, but Alexei Petrovich remained . . .

I went to bed in a terrible excitement, feeling a sense of dignity for the first time: someone loves me, I'm getting married. . . . Beyond that I couldn't make sense of the thoughts in my head. The next morning, I started getting ready to go to the music teacher, as usual, but my mother's maid told me with a smile,

"Young lady, your mama has ordered you not to go to your lessons today. . . . Congratulations, young lady!" she added significantly.

"On what?" I asked, shuddering.

"Don't be coy, young lady! After all, I heard Alexei Petrovich talking to your mama. You're a bride now. . . . So make me a gift of your old cloak."

Stepanida Petrovna was still in bed and seemed to be asleep. We were talking quietly, but at the word "bride" she jumped up, looked around in fright, and let out a wild scream: "Who? What bride?"

I signaled the maid to be quiet. My aunt grew agitated. I started looking at her the way I had the previous day.

"Why aren't you going to your lessons? It's already half past nine," she said uneasily.

"I don't feel like it," I said contemptuously.

She was growing more and more confused, but when Alexandra Semyonovna joyfully congratulated me, Stepanida Petrovna trembled and collapsed into a chair. . . . Her legs had given out. She buried her face in her hands and began to cry.

Suddenly the nursery was bustling, and a dull murmur was heard: "Mama is coming! Mama!" We heard firm footsteps from the hallway, and then Mama majestically entered the nursery. I kissed her hand and returned to my seat. She began, "Very good!

So this is how you carry on? I know everything." She tilted her head to the side, which endowed her entire figure with a stronger expression of maternal pride. "You're lucky to have us as parents," she continued. "Do you think he's marrying you for your face? No, out of respect for your father and mother." Changing her stately tone to one of simple condescension, she concluded, "Why didn't you tell me he wanted to marry you? Hm?"

"Because I haven't seen you at all . . ."

Somewhat taken aback by my bold answer, Mama answered tragically, "Well then, it's all settled now! I hope that you may live together as happily as your mother and father."

I couldn't help whispering, "God forbid!"

Noticing my lips moving, Mama asked angrily, "What?"

I kept silent. Seeing such indifference in her daughter, she hurried to finish the scene, which seemed to promise her a much greater effect.

"Well, congratulations—and here is my blessing for you!" She made a cross in the air and expressively extended her hand to me. But something, I don't know what, kept me from kissing it. Alexandra Semyonovna silently implored me but in vain: some new, strange feeling in me became louder and louder, and I did not move. Offended, my mother finished by pressing her rejected and tired hand to her chest, looking me up and down with contempt, and quickly leaving the nursery, channeling her remaining self-importance into her gait.

My brothers and sisters heralded my bravery; Alexandra Semyonovna scolded me and groaned. Stepanida Petrovna sat like a dead woman, her head bowed. Her braid was loose, and she stared senselessly at a comb she held in her hands. From time to time, her gaze fell on me. At last, she dressed and left the room in a hurry.

That evening, when Alexei Petrovich arrived, Papa brought him to the nursery and said, "Here's your bridegroom!"

And nothing else.

The engagement had occurred in a very unusual way, as Alexei Petrovich later told me. At first Mama could not conceal her surprise that he wanted to marry me, but she corrected herself: "However, don't look at her now—if you dress her up, she'll be very pretty . . ."

Alexei Petrovich asked her to keep the proposal a secret for the time being. She promised but later that day went and told her friends about the great respect she was being paid: a rich man, a nobleman, was marrying her daughter, and her other daughter had a betrothed, though not so rich, but of extraordinary intelligence and scholarly acumen.

The next day, while Alexandra Semyonovna was brushing her hair, Mama said to her, "Who does she think she is? Don't I have any authority over them? I'm their mother! I may be a musician's wife, but I'm not in raptures over that Alexei Petrovich, even if he is a nobleman. Who knows if he's telling the truth: his estate might just be a backwater with five hungry souls . . ."[1] She burst out laughing. "Perhaps our little noblewomen will come running back to their mother and father for a piece of bread. . . . Tell those girls I'll throw them out. . . . They won't get a thing from me!" And she got so worked up, as if her daughters were already standing before her in rags, surrounded by a bunch of hungry children with outstretched hands.

Grandpa clutched his calendar ever more tightly, informing everyone of my betrothed's morals, inclinations, and future fate. Grandma happily poured herself another drink. Uncle Semyon kissed me on the forehead for the first time and said, "Congratulations, *Mamselle* Na-ta-lya!"

Stepanida Petrovna did not come home; she stayed with Grandma and wrote a letter to Mama reproaching her for their younger sister's union with the son of the important man, the tyrannical treatment she endured, and much more. Mama took her anger out on Grandma.

At last, Sofia got engaged. Mama declared that she could offer no dowry to either of us, and we began to consider the matter together. When Alexei Petrovich gave me a present, Mama came to the nursery and told Auntie sweetly, "Look at this gift Kirilo Kirilych has given me. Yes, indeed, not a noble gift; it only cost three hundred rubles . . ." Finally, she called us to her and solemnly handed us each three hundred rubles in the smallest banknotes, so that the bundles seemed quite large, and an old silk dress. I did not want to accept either of these but was afraid to cause a new scene.

Ivan managed to tell Grandpa all sorts of fibs about our bridegrooms. That evening, when Auntie was pouring out tea, the old man sat down by her and said, "You're sitting there, don't know a thing, and you think to yourself, things are not what they used to be. In my day a general was an old man, but today they make you a general when you've hardly grown whiskers!"

"What general are you talking about, Pyotr Akimych?"

"Who else? Haven't you seen him? He's so thin . . ."

Grandpa thought my betrothed was a general.

Chapter Twelve

MEANWHILE, OUR UNCLE practically lived with us: cards had taken possession of him.

Once, Grandma came running to our house.

"Hello, my dears! What am I to do with Semyon? He's after some rat all the time! He went to bed and slept for two days straight. Doesn't eat anything, doesn't drink, his eyes are big, huge. . . . And those damn cards, Natasha! A month ago, he lost at cards, brought home a pawn ticket, counted all his money, and after that I never saw it again. . . . My God! What punishment! I'm frightened to go home. He says, 'Mama, look, there's a rat running around,' and, by God, Natasha, there is no rat. . . . He sneaks around trying to catch it—turns everything upside down, yelling at me all the while: 'You're keeping me from catching it,' he says, 'You're feeding them to me! That's why I don't eat anymore . . .' What? He's gone utterly mad! At first, I thought he was joking, but he looks so wild it gives me the chills!"

We begged Grandma to stay for dinner.

That evening, in the hallway, the dog started barking terribly. I ran over and saw my uncle. After throwing everyone's fur coats off the rack and making a mountain of them in the middle of the room, he carefully stretched his own coat across the entire rack. The dog passionately protected the fur coats under her guard. Uncle Semyon tried to soothe her, politely asking for her paw, but, wheezing and gasping, she stood on her hind legs and nearly choked on her collar. I petted her and she wagged her tail, but she continued her low growl, giving our uncle a wild look.

"Don't go near Trésor, Uncle! She'll bite you!"

"Don't worry, *Mamselle* Natalya. A rat's already bitten my finger. Hurts like the devil!" Uncle's face contorted horribly, then he smiled. "Well, I'll teach this dog a lesson . . ." He winked at me and let out a wild laugh. "She won't bite me after this!"

"Uncle, don't stand here. Let's go to the nursery."

"No, I'm going to the drawing room." Lowering his voice, he asked mysteriously, "Are they playing cards?"

"Yes, Uncle."

"Hm!" He went hesitantly to the drawing room.

I stood at the door and watched him.

Mama, Kirilo Kirilych, and Papa were playing Boston. Uncle Semyon sat down at the table without greeting anyone. He watched the game closely and burst into wild laughter whenever anyone made a mistake. A new game was dealt out. Kirilo Kirilych made his bid, blundered, and lost. Uncle reached across the table, calmly took aim, and flicked him on the forehead, shouting, "Fool! After all, the Queen has already come out!"

He showed his hand and stared at the fatal Queen. Kirilo Kirilych looked at his assailant in stupefaction. Semyon was silent, but his eyes, still fixed on the Queen, were unusually large. At last, he broke the silence by talking about the rats that had stolen his money.

"What are you talking about, Semyon? Are you well?" asked Mama, worried.

"Ha, ha, ha! I'm ill! No, I'm sorry! I want to rid myself of my old sins. . . . I shall ask forgiveness from everyone, everyone. . . . That's how it ought to be. . . . Isn't that right?"

The last question was directed to Kirilo Kirilych. Without waiting for an answer, Uncle Semyon went into the hallway.

He took it into his head again to pet Trésor, who bit and ripped the end of his shirt.

"Confound it! You pet this dog and she bites you! Is my father here?"

"Yes."

"Call him. I want to talk to him."

Grandpa entered the room, surprised.

"Hello, Semyon! What do you care for the father you drove —"

"Hello, Father," his son interrupted him affectionately.

Grandpa forgot his grievances.

"Forgive me, Father!"

Semyon fell at his father's feet. Grandpa jumped around him in fright and looked at us strangely, as if seeking an explanation for such an incredible event.

Uncle rose to his feet, tears streaming down his pale cheeks. He approached his father timidly.

"Have you forgiven me, Father?"

"God be with you, Semyon."

Grandpa waved his long arms, which almost hit the ceiling, and wiped his tears with his sleeve.

"Give me your hand, Father."

"What is it, Semyon, what for?"

Grandpa backed away from him.

"Give your son your hand!" said Semyon pathetically.

Grandpa involuntarily obeyed. Semyon kissed his hand reverently and, with pompous solemnity, left the nursery.

We were amazed by our uncle's sensitivity, and Grandpa could not believe his own good fortune. His tongue started wagging in a frenzy.

Four days later, our uncle went definitively mad. He ran into the nursery without a cap. His face was blue, his voice weak.

"Save me, for God's sake, save me! The rats will eat me, they even chased me down the street . . ." His sobs prevented him from finishing.

I felt sorry for him. Where was our formidable uncle who wasn't afraid of anyone or anything? Now he was trembling and crying, as his poor nephew once trembled and cried before him!

"Uncle, don't cry! Stay with us," I told him.

He raised his head, looked at me affectionately and said softly, "All right, Natasha, I'll stay." But suddenly he sighed and asked, frightened, "And my mother! Your mother? Kirilo Kirilych?"

The next day he was tricked into going to an asylum. It was no simple business. Papa suggested that they go hunting and

Semyon agreed. Dressed in a hunting outfit, with his huge boots, he made us laugh despite ourselves.

"Goodbye," he said cockily, pacing the room. "I'm going hunting! I'll take Trésor along. It's a pity they haven't given me my gun yet. I could try to kill at least one rat."

He died soon after.

Grandpa didn't want to believe that his son had gone mad.

"Why are you trying to convince me otherwise? Just recently he kissed my hand!"

"He was mad then, too."

"Nonsense, I don't believe it! Says, 'Forgive me, Father.' Would a madman say that? He even bowed at my feet. . . . No, don't talk nonsense."

Uncle's madness was a great shock. I even forgot my impending wedding, though my mother reminded me of it by reproaching me for not fulfilling various customs: Why didn't I wear an engagement ring; why didn't I sew myself a satin wedding dress? She used Sofia, who strictly followed all the customs, as an example.

On the eve of the wedding, when we were packing my suitcase to go straight from the church to the village, my mother appeared in the nursery, blessed me again, shed tears, and sealed my forehead with a farewell kiss.

On my wedding day, I dressed very simply in a white muslin dress with a high bodice. I combed my hair smooth and wore not a single ribbon, nor any jewelry or accessories. Auntie was horrified.

"Oh, my God! Alexei Petrovich will be ashamed to marry such a bride. Please, at least put on my turquoise earrings!"

But I didn't.

The clock struck noon. I went out into the drawing room, where my mother and father awaited me with an icon, bread, and salt. Grandpa was wearing his formal clothes: a white kerchief that hid his customary tie; a canary-colored vest; and a blue tailcoat with gold buttons, a waist that rode up to his shoulder blades, and tails that fell to his heels. The collar of Grandpa's coat hid the back of his head. He could not turn it or see anything to the side, just like a horse with blinders. His tight pink demi-cotton pantaloons hugged his skinny, sky-high legs. His boots were so creaky that when he walked it seemed as though he were playing the accordion.

"Where are the guests?" he asked in surprise. They told him there wouldn't be any. He took offense.

But instead of guests, the room soon filled with household members who came to see how I would be sent to the altar. Even Trésor, taking advantage of the commotion, with a rope around her neck, quietly crept under the table, where she watched the whole ceremony with visible pleasure.

They began to bless me. On my aunt's order, I kissed the icon and bowed to the ground. Then the farewells began.

"Goodbye, may you live happily!" my father said confidently and calmly, handing over his daughter for life to a man he knew only by name. Mama played the scene like a tragedy.

Auntie cried so much that I also burst into tears. She loved us. I also felt, in that moment, that I loved her . . .

Vanya, moved by our tears, whispered to me, "Now you're crying, too, Natasha?"

I wiped away my tears.

"Goodbye, Natasha!" said Grandma, who had already started drinking from grief. "Give your grandmother a hug!"

I hugged her but didn't feel particularly sad to say goodbye to her.

"Goodbye, Grandpa!" I said.

"Goodbye, Natasha! Don't forget: in September he will be content in all things; October is not a good month for him; February . . ."

"All right, all right, Grandpa. Goodbye!"

"No, listen to me: in February he should buy and sell . . ."

"That's enough, Pyotr Akimych," shouted Grandma. "Don't bother her with your nonsense!"

He rushed to her angrily.

"Well! I suppose you don't like it? You don't like it because it's true. You're a spendthrift, a nag, a blabbermouth!" And he told his wife the same old story . . .

Meanwhile, I said goodbye to my brothers and sisters. My heart sank. . . . It was hardest for me to part with Vanya; I don't know why. Perhaps because we always shared our grief with each other, even though he was much younger than me.

"Vanya, don't be naughty."

"Now I can if I want to: Uncle's gone!"

"Well, goodbye."

And I kissed him again.

"Natasha, kiss Liza again!"

Vanya lifted her up to me, and I fulfilled his wish. My father appeared in the doorway in his fur coat.

"It's time; we'll be late!"

Sobbing, I kissed everyone again and ran out into the hallway. They wanted to follow me, but my father forbade them, fearing that more farewells would delay us. Grandpa waved his long arms and shouted after me, "Remember, Natasha, the months of October and March, too . . ."

Only Trésor, with a rope around her neck, accompanied me to the carriage.

"Goodbye, Trésor!"

In response she gently wagged her tail at me.

"Goodbye, young lady," said Luka, lifting me into the carriage. "I wish you every happiness."

My father also climbed in, and the doors slammed shut. As the carriage drove off, I took one last look at the house where I had shed so many tears. The windows were dotted with heads. Grandpa kept waving at me. Everyone bowed to me, and I bowed, too. But soon everything disappeared, and only Trésor, with the rope around her neck, sat dejectedly on the porch, watching the carriage disappear.

■ ■ ■

Here ends the manuscript that chanced to fall into my hands. What became of its cast of characters, I do not know. At one point in her notes, the heroine calls herself an old woman. It follows from this that the events described do not relate to the present time. In fact, many of the events of the writer's childhood will simply not be believed today. In any case, if these notes, with their pointed description of the coarseness and depravity of an upbringing at the hands of parents who are negligent and morally bereft, force people to look more closely at themselves and shame those who are guilty in this regard before their children and before society, then this, I think, shall serve a sufficient reason to print them.

ACKNOWLEDGMENTS

I AM SO HAPPY to thank my own collective of collaborators. Thank you to Margarita Vaysman, Hilde Hoogenboom, and Anna Berman for sharing your expertise in all matters of nineteenth-century Russian women's writing. Nora Seligman Favorov, I am so grateful for your close reading and historical sleuthing, undertaken with the gracious help of Rimma Garn. The generous financial support of the Yale Translation Initiative supported my work on this project. To the members of the Yale Literary Translation Collective, including Rose FitzPatrick, Sam Karagulin, Lora Maslenitsyna, Jacob Romm, and Emily Ziffer, thank you for years of friendship and line edits. Natalia Black, thank you for all those summertime conversations about the material history of Panaeva's world and, especially, for your good-humored explanations of her jokes. Thank you to Marian Schwartz for our correspondence, which always leaves me thinking more about translation and the virtue of not taking things too seriously. Nathan Katkin, thank you for your honest and witty comments. Mari Jarris, thank you for teaching me about Panaeva's friend, Nikolai Chernyshevsky, and for being a perspicacious reader in the best sense. Venya Gushchin, you are so generous with brilliant feedback and words of encouragement. Katya Olson Shipyatsky, thank you for always pointing me back to the stakes of this work. To Samuel Page, who has the wit of Panaeva and the optimism of Vera Pavlovna, thank you for your careful attention. Finally, thank you to Kristin Crance and Liam Bell for thinking and rethinking family with me. You all have made *The Talnikov Family*, and its questions of love and liberation, feel freshly urgent. I'm so thankful to Christine Dunbar and her colleagues at Columbia University Press for taking up this urgency and guiding Panaeva's novel into the hands of English-language readers.

NOTES

INTRODUCTION

1. Avdotia Panaeva, *Vospominaniia* (Moscow: Khudozhestvennaia literatura, 1972), 170.
2. Panaeva, *Vospominaniia*, 171–72.
3. I. S. Turgenev, *Polnoe sobranie sochinenii i pisem v tridtsati tomakh* (Moscow: Nauka, 1978, Volume 3, page 232).
4. Jehanne M. Gheith and Beth Holmgren, "Art and Prostokvasha: Avdot'ia Panaeva's Work," in *The Russian Memoir: History and Literature*, ed. Beth Holmgren (Evanston, IL: Northwestern University Press, 2003), 138.
5. Jehanne M. Gheith, "Redefining the Perceptible: The Journalism(s) of Evgeniia Tur and Avdot'ia Panaeva," in *An Improper Profession: Women, Gender, and Journalism in Late Imperial Russia*, ed. Barbara T. Norton and Jehanne M. Gheith (Durham, NC: Duke University Press, 2001).
6. Panaeva, *Vospominaniia*, 175.
7. The only other full English-language translation of Panaeva's work is the novella *The Young Lady of the Steppes*, in *Russian Women's Shorter Fiction: An Anthology 1835–1860*, trans. Joe Andrew (Oxford: Clarendon, 1996).
8. Margarita Vaysman, *Self-Conscious Realism: Metafiction and the Nineteenth-Century Russian Novel* (Cambridge: Legenda, 2021); Colleen Lucey, *Love*

NOTES

for Sale: Representing Prostitution in Imperial Russia (Ithaca, NY: Northern Illinois University Press, 2021), 123.
9. Gheith and Holmgren, "Art and Prostokvasha," 132.
10. Panaeva, *Vospominaniia*, 267.

CHAPTER 1

1. Russian names often take diminutive forms that suggest the speaker's felt intimacy with the person being named or the speaker's social seniority. This novel, with its many children's characters, features many such diminutives: for example, the narrator's full name is Natalya, but she goes by Natasha because she is a child. Her siblings Ekaterina, Sofia, Mikhail, Fedor, and Ivan are regularly called Katya, Sonya, Misha, Fedya, and Vanya (and this beloved youngest brother sometimes earns the more emphatic diminutive form "Vanyusha"). Natasha respectfully refers to adult characters by their first names and patronymics (the patronymic is derived from the name of the person's father). Elena Petrovna and Stepanida Petrovna are sisters, both daughters of Pyotr.
2. Willow Week, also known as Catkin Week, is the week before Holy Week (the final week of Lent, ending with Easter Sunday) in the Russian Orthodox calendar.

CHAPTER 2

1. The phrases mean "Allow me to leave" and "Pardon me."

CHAPTER 3

1. Mama uses the magenta juice of garden beets as blush. Panaeva refers to the rise of sugar beet production in Russia from the 1820s to the 1840s, an alternative to imported cane sugar.
2. Raised in a household of actors, Panaeva was steeped in the European repertoire. Natasha, too, frequently compares people to characters in plays. Here she likely references Friedrich Schiller's 1800 verse play *Mary Stuart*, in which Mary's neck is praised (before her beheading).

- 164 -

3. The Cossacks were a multiethnic group of seminomadic warriors who lived around the Black and Caspian Seas. Famous for their independence, fierceness, and horsemanship, they figure prominently in the Russian cultural imagination as ethnically othered (typically Ukrainian) social outsiders.
4. Stepanida and Elena are performing a Russian Christmastime folk practice in which young women divine the name of their future husbands. In a famous scene in *Eugene Onegin* (1833), Pushkin's heroine Tatiana engages in the same ritual.
5. Figaro is the crafty, insubordinate hero of a trilogy of comic plays by Pierre Beaumarchais, later adapted in operas by Rossini and Mozart.

CHAPTER 5

1. Semyon sings lines from the folk song "On the Mother Neva River" (*Kak na matushke na Neve reke*).

CHAPTER 6

1. The shakes are a colloquial term for delirium tremens (DTs), a set of alcohol withdrawal symptoms including shaking, sweating, and hallucinations.
2. Whenever Grandpa closes the chimney to conserve heat, the apartment fills with carbon monoxide and causes Grandma's headaches.
3. Bruce's Calendar was an eighteenth-century Russian almanac named after James Bruce (1669–1735), a Russian scientist and military commander of Scottish descent. Reprinted throughout this period, the calendar featured astronomical, religious, and geographical information, as well as prophecies and omens.
4. The courtyards of urban buildings were typically guarded, but this one clearly did not employ a watchman.
5. Grandma chides the intruder for failing to abstain from meat on Wednesday, one of the fasting days (along with Friday) in Russian Orthodox practice.
6. Given that Ivan Panaev knew English and even translated new English-language works into Russian to share with his wife (including

Jane Eyre in 1847), it is possible that Edgar Allan Poe's 1843 short story "The Tell-Tale Heart" is an intertext in this scene.

CHAPTER 7

1. Grandpa refers to a Russian folktale about a stubborn married couple: a husband tells his wife he has shaved his beard, but she insists that it's only been trimmed. They continue to argue over this technicality until the husband begins drowning the wife. Submerged underwater, she raises two fingers out of the water, like scissors, to insist that his beard was trimmed. This story was recorded as "The Quarrelsome Wife" (*Zhena-sporshchitsa*) by the ethnographer Alexander Afanasyev (1855–1867) in his *Russian Folktales*.

2. Luka was likely an enserfed aide to a nobleman officer during the Russo-Turkish War of 1806–1811.

3. Luka and the narrator use the racial slur *zhid* ("Yid") and the feminine variant, *zhidovka*. I have chosen not to reproduce these slurs in the main text, opting instead for the terms "Jew" and "Jewish girl." Nevertheless, this scene is a striking rehearsal of Russian racializing discourse. Luka's is an orientalist tale, recounted in the language of a Russian peasant, about the supposed wildness of Jewish women. Natasha declares at the end of this scene, "We had trouble falling asleep that night and had terrible dreams." The reason for her terror is unclear: the "savagery" of the Jewish woman, the cruelty of Luka's master, or both?

CHAPTER 8

1. The family is "sitting before the road," a Russian tradition in which a group sits in silence before anyone begins a trip.

CHAPTER 10

1. The Savior Church on Haymarket Square, constructed in the mid-eighteenth century and demolished in 1961, features prominently in Dostoevsky's 1866 novel *Crime and Punishment*.

NOTES

2. *The Ice Palace* (*Ledianoi dom*) was a popular historical novel, written in 1835 by Ivan Lazhechnikov, about love and intrigue in the court of Empress Anna in the 1730s.

CHAPTER 11

1. Enserfed people were commonly referred to as "souls" in nineteenth-century Russia.

www.ingramcontent.com/pod-product-compliance
Lightning Source LLC
LaVergne TN
LVHW040538311224
800286LV00003B/337